CW00729370

Roddy Murray

George Milne –

Murder at the

Butler's Convention

Acknowledgements

I big thank you to Sandy Murray and Margaret Rustad for their help and assistance with the text and storyline. A thank you to Linda Wilson-Bell for her advice on Equine matters.

A thank you to everyone who read George Milne- Cat Detective for their comments and advice.

As ever a huge thank you to Pauline MacGillivray for her constant support.

By the same author;

Body and Soul

The Treasure Hunters

George Milne – Cat Detective

A Snow White Scenario

For my parents and for my children.

Chapter One: Favourite Chair

George Milne sat on his favourite chair and took stock of his life. He knew that he was happy now in a way that he could never have imagined while he was married to Glenda. In fact, just being happy instead of miserable was a huge step forward. He lived with Janine now and enjoyed all of the matrimonial bliss which had been denied him in the past. He had no financial worries ever since being left with Frankie Cook's emergency suitcase containing all that money. As part and parcel of acquiring the money he had taken seriously the responsibility of looking after Frankie's sister Evelyn. She may have wanted nothing but she wanted for nothing anyway. Most important of all to Evelyn, was the fact that she was safe now and had the companionship of Janine's daughter Rosie and her girlfriend Carol. This had created stability and a feeling of belonging which had never fully existed in her life before she met George.

As an indirect consequence of this happy set-up, George's favourite chair was no longer a chair. Gone were the days when he would sit alone and watch television with a cup of tea and a chocolate digestive as the highlight of his day to look forward to. Instead, his favourite chair was now the sofa, and he liked nothing better than to curl up on it with Janine in the evenings watching television. He would usually get to watch the news but thereafter the programmes were irrelevant to him. The main thing was curling up with Janine. Occasionally Rosie would join them with Carol. This meant Evelyn would come along too, still too fragile to be left on her own in the flat which they shared. It was not uncommon then for George to find himself squashed on the sofa between his lovely Janine, her equally lovely daughter, her partner and their flatmate, all dressed in matching onesies. Life could not get better he would think to himself at such times, as an unidentified piece of femininity brushed against his leg.

He had largely given up his old Cat Detective business. He placed no adverts and had stopped giving out business cards. If distraught owners phoned him though, to plead for his help in tracking down their lost, much loved cat, he would still allow them the comfort brought by handing him two hundred pounds. Beyond that he did nothing further. Sometimes the cat would return; often it would not. Either way he was never responsible for the owners' joy or sorrow and that suited him fine. He didn't like the awesome responsibility of expectation. He sold hope now and nothing else.

Chapter Two: Lola Cortez

One evening, when George had been looking forward to another average, quiet scrum on the couch, Carol's phone made that infuriating sound half way between a wolf whistle and a canary being strangled which indicated the receipt of a text. Carol announced to everyone assembled on the couch that she had just received a message from her friend Lola Cortez. She had met Lola in Spain and they had travelled round part of Europe together for a few years. Nobody asked the obvious question regarding exactly how close they had been, but it was clear they had been great friends in a past life.

George paid no attention to the announcement. He already had more than enough women in his life, including one who actually slept with him. Instead he continued to watch the news. He therefore missed the discussions centred round Lola visiting Carol and Rosie and also the suggestion from Janine that she would be better off staying in George's spare room for the duration of the visit rather than trying to squeeze into the spare room in Evelyn's flat along with Rosie and Carol.

"That would be okay, wouldn't it, George?" asked Janine.

"Sure, no problem," agreed George without any idea of what he had agreed to.

Chapter Three: Lola makes her entrance

Despite the cramped conditions, it had been decided that Lola would spend her first night in Coatshill at the flat with Rosie, Carol and Evelyn. It was reasoned that the girls would probably be up all night talking and the sleeping arrangements would take care of themselves when they all finally crashed out. Thereafter, though, she would move into George's spare room as he had apparently agreed. She could then walk round to the flat as and when she liked to spend time with the other girls. This had all made sense to Janine at the time she had agreed it.

They were made aware of the fact that Lola had arrived via a confirmatory text from Rosie, and the following day Janine prepared the spare room accordingly. Thirty minutes after the appointed hour, George's doorbell rang and both he and Janine rose from the sofa and opened the front door to their guest. Neither were sure exactly what to expect but both were surprised anyway by Lola's appearance. Despite the inclement weather hitting Lanarkshire from the direction of Russia, Lola was dressed in a short flamenco-style dress which plunged dangerously at the neckline. She wore shoes which would have been perfect for dancing indoors but nothing else, and dragged behind her a small airline style suitcase which presumably contained all her worldly possessions. How she survived with so little in tow was hinted at when the taxi driver asked who was paying the fare. As ever George felt obliged and cleared the amount with a very small tip. Janine and George exchanged looks before welcoming Lola indoors and encouraging her to sit close to the gas fire.

On closer inspection they noticed that although well preserved and dressed like a young girl heading to Torremolinos for her first unaccompanied holiday, Lola was halfway between their ages and Rosie's, in other words somewhere in her mid-thirties. She declined both tea and coffee but agreed to have a glass of wine to keep the others company.

After failing to engage her in any meaningful conversation, Janine showed her to the spare room, pointing out the bathroom and kitchen on the way. It looked like it might have happened anyway, but when invited to make herself at home, Lola promptly collapsed on the bed and immediately fell asleep. Janine removed the younger women's shoes and loosened the dress, noticing as she did so that Lola was not wearing a bra, and gently pulled the throw over her.

"Strange woman," said Janine as she re-joined George in the front room. "Not what I expected at all really, although I'm not sure what I did expect."

"Same here," said George, playing safe but without being any more specific.

Janine had a long-standing engagement for an evening out organised with an old school friend, and after the two had eaten a light meal she went through to the main bedroom and changed. After that she put on what George described as her war paint, having heard somebody laugh at the expression once, then went into the front room to say goodbye.

"Will you be okay here?" she asked, a little concerned without quite knowing why. "It might be difficult to keep a conversation going till I get back."

"I expect she'll sleep through till the morning if she was up gabbing all night with Carol and Rosie," replied George.

"I suppose so," said Janine. She kissed George on the forehead from behind the sofa and told him to have a nice evening before adding in his ear, "It might well be worth your while waiting up for me."

George gave a thumbs-up without looking round and Janine left, still feeling slightly uneasy.

The evening started very much as George had anticipated, with peace, perfect peace to watch the darts tournament on the television and then the re-runs of the previous Saturday's celebrity dance-off, including interviews with the celebrities and their professional dance partners. At about eleven o'clock or so, George couldn't remember exactly when for some reason, Lola appeared again in the living room. The second thing George noticed about her was that she appeared to be completely refreshed after what could only have been a few hours' sleep at best. It was the second thing he noticed because the first thing that he noticed was that Lola wasn't wearing a stitch of clothing.

"I hope you don't mind George but I hate wearing clothes when I'm indoors. It is just so restrictive," said Lola in her Spanish accent.

George didn't mind one little bit and indicated so by saying nothing whatsoever. His jaw would have bounced off the carpet if it hadn't been attached firmly to his face.

"What are you watching?" she asked George, who had mainly been watching Lola as she sat down on one of the arm chairs and crossed her legs.

"Just the dancing programme. It's a repeat," George managed to say without stuttering.

"I love to dance," Said Lola. "It keeps everything so firm, don't you think?"

As if to provide proof, she stood up, did a little twirl and sat down again. George had to agree that everything looked very firm to him.

"It makes sex and living so much easier when you keep things firm."

George merely nodded, unable to find a flaw in Lola's logic even though he had no intention of searching for one.

"Would you like a tea or coffee?" George enquired.

"Any more of that wine? I find caffeine unhealthy."

"Yes, I'll just get the bottle from the kitchen," said George. Before he could rise to his feet, however, Lola had bounced onto her toes and pirouetted to the door laughing as she went.

George watched every graceful movement, enjoying the live dance show far more than the repeats on his television. After all, the girls in the programme were fully dressed.

Lola returned after a few minutes with the opened wine bottle and two glasses.

"Will you join me, George? I so hate to drink alone, although I never let it stop me."

George took the glass from her hand and tried desperately to keep it steady as Lola filled it to the top.

"Wouldn't you be more comfortable wearing something?" asked George after a moment or two when Lola had again sat down and crossed her legs. He had suddenly become conscious of the fact that Janine would be home quite soon and he felt obliged to at least try to neutralise the scene she would find waiting for her.

"No thank you. I much prefer to remain as nature intended. Please don't be embarrassed! Feel free to look at me if you like, or even join me."

George declined, convinced of two things: Lola would not want to look at him too much if he was naked, and Janine would immediately kill him if she found him alone and naked with Lola. As it was, the situation was starting to worry him.

"Would you mind too much if I turned the fire up just a little? I have still not adjusted fully to the Scottish climate."

George offered to do better than that and turned the controls of the central heating up a notch or two. To hell with the cost, he thought to himself. This had required him to turn around on the sofa and reach round for the control on the wall. As he turned back he discovered Lola bending over in front of him and switching on the remaining bar of the fire before starting to dance in time to the music on the television. Again his mouth fell open, but he was unable to speak.

As Lola swayed to the beat with the glass of wine in her hand, George heard the front door open with a key and knew that Janine was home. He looked at the tableau which awaited her in the living room. None of it was his fault, he reasoned. Their house guest had appeared without clothing and had declined his suggestion to put something on. She had also produced the second wine glass uninvited. Yes, he was in the clear.

Janine walked into the living room and stopped dead in her tracks. She saw Lola immediately she entered the room and George a split second afterwards. Lola was dancing round the room naked whilst demonstrating what appeared to be flamenco. George shrugged his shoulders as if to say don't blame me. Janine didn't, for now.

"Ah, Janine, I was just saying to George how I adore to dance. I hope you don't mind me wearing nothing. It is my habit and you did say make yourself at home. George was kind enough to put the heating up for me"

"I bet he was," whispered Janine under her breath.

Then Janine smiled and used her years of experience working in bars to assist Lola out of the room at speed without her feeling either unwelcome or that she had any choice in the matter.

George hid his disappointment as he watched and again smiled at Janine, hoping she read it as a thanks for saving his embarrassment. There was no confirmation in her manner suggesting she saw things in this way, but it was the best he could manage after what had been an unusual evening.

After fifteen minutes or so both women returned with Lola now wearing a onesie and Janine put the fire and central heating down several notches to prevent Lola being tempted to strip again.

George was watching the news by now and Janine knew that he would be engrossed - perhaps not quite as engrossed as he had been watching a naked young woman demonstrate her dancing skills, but engrossed enough to re-establish some semblance of normality.

"I have explained to Lola the house rules here which include being dressed or at least fully covered at all times in the public areas."

George looked up from the news and nodded. "Probably best all round," was all he managed, but he could tell that the blame had been placed squarely with their houseguest and that the night might yet include the promised romantic conclusion with Janine. After watching Lola walk around his house naked he rather hoped it would. It had put him in the mood, to say the least, and the smile on Janine's face suggested she could already see the funny side. Lola grew bored and tired quite quickly after that and headed back to her bedroom.

When the news finished, Janine rose to her feet and, moving towards the doorway of the lounge, raised her skirt at the back.

"Would you like to see me dirty dancing?" she asked George.

George nodded and followed her, thinking that he rather thought he would.

<u>Chapter Four: Lola Cortez</u>

Lola Cortez had been born and christened Theresa Maguire in the Drumchapel district of Glasgow. Her mother had given birth almost exactly nine months after a holiday in the Spanish resort of Lloret de Mar. Theresa never knew her father and suspected in later life that her mother may not have been too certain either as to who he was. What she did grow up knowing was that her mother loved Spain, loved the Spanish people and language and loved Spanish men in particular. As a result, the two of them took several holidays in Spain each year during the first ten years or so of Theresa's life.

On one of these holidays, Theresa's mother Margaret met and fell in love with a Spaniard called Miguel. That particular holiday lasted some six years as Margaret moved in with Miguel and helped him run his café-bar in Torremolinos. Theresa was started at the local school, where she quickly made friends and learned the language as school-age children do. She found the weather and lifestyle a huge change for the better after Drumchapel and determined that she would become as Spanish as she possibly could.

When her mother married Miguel and took his family name of Cortez, Theresa was delighted and immediately started using the name herself. In her mind that only left the Theresa part to deal with. Inspiration came from an unexpected direction. The bar was a lively one with, unusually, a mix of both Spanish and British regulars almost all of whom worked in the resort one way or another. As the season came to an end, the bar would fill each evening with an eclectic mix of people, determined to relax and have fun. One of the favourite activities on such occasions was the karaoke.

One evening, late in the year, when the resort was empty of holidaymakers and the bar was full of locals, Theresa was watching the usual suspects taking their turns at the karaoke. She was just about to head off to bed voluntarily, so bad was the standard that night, when her mother and Miguel appeared from the stock room, where they had changed into bizarre costumes. Miguel wore a pair of tight flared trousers, a sweater and a huge false nose. Margaret was wearing a sequined leotard, high heeled shoes and a feather headdress. There was also a tail made of feathers stuck to her bottom. Theresa stared at her mother in wonder; she had never seen such a beauty in all her life.

Miguel nodded to his brother Tony who was always master of ceremonies and he put on a song which must have been arranged in advance. Theresa had never heard it before but all the adults seemed to know it and started singing 'Copacabana' along with Barry Manilow. Margaret and Miguel danced and acted out the parts as the song played in the background. Miguel played the part of Tony in the song with conviction but all eyes were on Margaret. She danced and twirled, high kicked and strutted round the bar. Theresa had never seen anything like it, and by the time the song finished and everyone cheered and clapped, she knew that she wanted to grow up and be Lola like her mother, with an audience cheering her and marvelling at her beauty.

For years afterwards, Margaret would find Theresa in her bedroom trying on the 'Lola' outfit; tripping over the tail feathers at first in the too big high heels but slowly growing to fill both the costume and the shoes as her body grew and blossomed. From the day following the Copacabana act in the pub, Theresa insisted that everyone called her Lola. The customers happily indulged her but her folks (and she now regarded Miguel as her dad), were resistant. She had a perfectly good name; the same one as her grandmother had had. If it was good enough for her… etc. After two years, however, they gave up and Theresa became Lola to them too.

Lola took to Spanish culture like a duck to water, taking Flamenco lessons and reading up on heroes and heroines alike. Tales of Moorish culture and the conquest of South America in particular struck a chord and instilled in her an unquenchable wanderlust. Torremolinos was a big improvement on Drumchapel but it lacked the imagined excitement to be had in North Africa, Peru or Mexico.

With her looks and itchy feet, it was only a matter of time before Lola launched herself at the world. The opportunity came when she was sixteen and at the age when all teenage girls become incapable of agreeing with their mothers. After a furious argument with Margaret regarding the time Lola had returned home the previous night, she packed an airline bag with clothes and disappeared during the following night with a Norwegian student heading for Marrakech.

After several days travelling, the pair ended up in Morocco where Lola was able to find work as a dancer in a tented show for tourists. Her flamenco lessons paid off, although she was actually employed to belly dance, something which she had to learn quickly, having lied about her abilities at the interview.

Lola realised later that Anders the Norwegian student must have left sometime shortly after she started dancing professionally, but she was unconcerned. He had provided the necessary ticket out of Smallville and she was now loose in the big world. The dancing job lasted a season and, turning down the offer of becoming the director's mistress, Lola headed north again and, via Gibraltar, headed for Portugal. She had some money left from her savings and pay but knew it wouldn't last forever, or cover the cost of travelling to South America. As a financial precaution to cover the lean winter months, she moved in with the foreman of a vineyard who had successfully chatted her up one night, to his great surprise. He was ill-mannered and unpleasant but the accommodation was free and he reluctantly accepted her refusal to do any household work. The arrangement lasted till Spring, when her natural love of dancing caused a fight in the local nightclub where she insisted on going every Friday night. Her foreman boyfriend was a reluctant dancer at best and found himself watching his much younger partner, on such occasions, dance well into the night with local young men. His patience would only last so long though, and when it ran out he would half drag Lola away to his home. On this particular Spring evening, Lola may have felt the first of many seasonal urges to migrate without realising it and danced most of the evening with a burly young lorry driver from Madrid.

The ensuing fight saw the vineyard go without its foreman for a week due to hospitalisation, which conveniently gave Lola the opportunity to recover her meagre belongings and travel by heavy goods vehicle to Spain's capital city.

She loved travel, but not necessarily in the cab of a Volvo truck, and so she swapped this option for a sports car to Paris. Clement was a successful salesman in his family's

French wines business and had money to burn. He lavished a lot of it on Lola as they took a week to travel to Paris and was heartbroken when she declined his spontaneous offer of marriage.

Lola loved Paris and found herself taken up by a fast crowd of wealthy youngsters who refused to play by their parents' rules; indeed, often by any rules at all. Having grown up helping to run a bar, she was never a heavy drinker but her insatiable curiosity led her to try everything else that life and her new friends had to offer. That opened a world of possibilities and Lola embraced it all.

After a few years in Paris, she had met Carol and the two women travelled round Europe together for some time. When the inevitable parting came, they promised to meet up again at some future date and compare tales of adventure. As a result of this promise, and needing free accommodation, Lola had made contact when she finally returned to her native Scotland.

Chapter Five: Lola and her Knife-throwing Act

Lola had eventually been persuaded to wear a onesie or at least some clothing or pyjamas whilst living under George and Janine's roof. Even George had reluctantly confirmed that it was a rule of the house, but only after Janine put her foot down for the first time since they had got together. So it was that George and Janine found themselves on the sofa one night watching Strictly Come Dancing with Rosie, Carol, Evelyn and Lola draped over the sofa, the surrounding floor, chairs and arms of the sofa itself.

"Tell me about this act of yours," Janine enquired pleasantly of Lola.

Up till that point Lola had not given any details of her time touring the world after parting with Carol, aside from the intriguing admission that it had recently included a stint with a Bulgarian circus. She had waved away questions previously, refusing to say anything beyond the fact that it hadn't worked out.

On this particular evening they had all had a few glasses of wine before, during and after their evening meal and Janine had correctly guessed that Lola was bored with the television programmes on offer.

Lola eyed up Janine and obviously decided the time was right to divulge further details of her life with the circus.

"It was great fun and the sights we saw were amazing. We would pitch tents in major cities, but we were also hired for private functions - billionaires, millionaires and politicians mainly. Especially Russians; gangsters, I expect, but they all had money to burn and if their daughters or trophy wives wanted a circus at their party, who were we to argue if cash was on offer? After each performance we would sit around the trailers smoking joints and talking endlessly till the adrenaline of performing subsided and we could sleep. I would often sleep with one of a troupe of tumblers who all had magnificent bodies. The catcher in the trapeze act was another of my favourites. I only once slept with a clown when there was nobody else available. After all, a cock is a cock."

Janine poured Lola another glass of wine noticing her Spanish accent occasionally revert back to Glaswegian as the drink flowed and she had to force herself not to laugh at Lola's complete lack of discretion.

"I had tried to work out enough to be a trapeze artist too but I had started too late in life. Instead I was the part of a knife-throwing act. A Romanian called Mike, for some reason, would throw 12 spangled knifes at me while I stood against a large wheel. For the grand finale, he would tie me to the wheel, spin it and then throw knives after being blindfolded by the ringmaster."

"That all sounds very exciting," encouraged Janine, who noticed that Rosie, Carol and especially Evelyn were now listening intently.

"It sounds exciting perhaps. Of course he could see through the blindfold. That's why the ringmaster had to put it on. It would have been obvious to the audience up close."

"So you were really quite safe."

"Safe," laughed Lola so loudly that George looked round from the television briefly before returning to the dancing competition on offer. "How can you be safe with a drunk who throws knives at you?"

"Were you ever hurt?" asked Evelyn with wide eyed excitement.

"No more than once a week," replied Lola gently. She had taken a sisterly liking to Evelyn. "One of the clowns, the one I slept with, was a magnificent medic and patched me up between performances. That's how I got to know him. Ultimately though I became worried for my looks and left the act. I had learned to throw the knives at least as well as Mike could. I suggested we changed the act so that we both came on as before, me stunning in leotard and feathers and Mike as usual carrying the knives. Just as the audience are expecting a standard knife throwing act I would take the knives, tie Mike to the wheel and throw them at him. Mike wasn't sure but would have done anything for me, one way or another. The circus manager wouldn't agree. He was a traditionalist and said it wasn't what the punters came to watch."

"It would have been a much better act," said Carol. "Girl-power and all that. You should go for it, even now."

"I missed my chance with the circus. Now I would need a new assistant. Someone like Mike who looked a bit long in the tooth and had gone to seed; someone who would lull the audience into a false sense of comfort as we came on. There are plenty of young folk I could persuade but it would be difficult to persuade an old trooper to slum it like that."

"But surely if all the person needs to do is stand and look worried it would be easy to find a volunteer. Put an advert in the paper," advised Carol warming to her theme.

"Older performers would see it as a form of failure to act as second fiddle to a woman. They wouldn't be interested till I had a booking."

"Why not try and get some bookings first, then advertise?" suggested Rosie.

"I would need to have a partner for any auditions with agencies. It is the old 'cart before the horse' thing."

George was miles away as usual. On the television it had just been announced that the elderly news reader competing with a professional dancer had not only been voted through to the next round of the dancing competition but had lost a further five pounds that week, taking his total weight loss to over three stones. George, along with the studio audience, was very impressed. The hapless anchor-man had not improved as a dancer beyond being considerably lighter on his feet, but he had been taken to the heart of the nation and they were rooting for him to win the overall prize. To George this was success indeed but he was also interested in the fact that the Russian professional dancer hugged the journalist and kissed him on the cheek each week the results and his weight loss were announced. That looked like a good job to George. It was also obvious that the two of them had to spend hours in each other's arms and occasionally in a heap together on the floor at rehearsals. That would be even more fun. George was so engrossed in the programme and the young Russian girl's costume that he was completely oblivious to the dangers heading his way.

"So all you would need is a middle-aged guy who looked like he had seen better days to walk on with you, hand you the knives and then stand still while you threw them at the wheel behind him," persisted Carol.

"Pretty much," said Lola. "I have all my own stuff in storage; the knives, costumes and the promise of a revolving wheel I could borrow from a friend who is a dominatrix in Edinburgh. That bit is easy; finding the stooge is the difficult thing."

George giggled at the newsreader's poor attempts at the tango with a still smiling Russian beauty at his side. He looked round to see if anyone else was enjoying the dancing as much as he was and found all the ladies in the room staring at him.

"It's quite an act," he said. Nobody replied at first.

"It would be the best act ever to make it to the stage," said Lola, confusing George slightly. He turned back to the safety of the television and left the girls to talk about onesies or knitting or whatever it had been they had been discussing. It had nothing to do with him.

Janine was unhappy with the term stooge but she could see the potential of George leading Lola onto the stage at a rehearsal to the groans of any agents present and then picture their faces as Lola took over and stole the show. At her stage of inebriation it seemed to make perfect sense that George would volunteer and get Lola as far as a few bookings. Thereafter it was over to her to find a suitable professional replacement for the actual gigs. It wouldn't break Janine's heart either, to wave Lola goodbye as she started on a world tour. She was just a bit too attractive and available to have anywhere near her man, even if it was George: perhaps especially if it was George. She still remembered the look on his face when Lola was dancing naked in their living room.

George was aware that he had been asked a question but such was his concentration on the television programme that he had missed exactly what he had been asked. Again he looked round to find five women staring at him but this time awaiting a response. It filtered through to his distracted brain that it had been Janine who had spoken. Logically that meant it must be a fairly straight forward question and he would do well to agree.

"Yes, no problem," he assured her.

There was a worrying pause and for a few seconds of panic George wondered if the correct response should have been 'No'.

The younger girls broke the silence with squeals and all gathered round to hug him. The alarm bells really started though when Evelyn said: "You are brave, George."

George desperately tried to retrace his steps and figure out what the question had been. Giving one of Janine's friends or one of the girls a lift was unlikely to require bravery, even in Evelyn's eyes. He smiled and found Janine smiling back. All was good then. He knew whatever it was had been approved of by her and he would be informed of any details later. Life was good. Now back to the dance-off. The newsreader appeared to be visibly losing weight by sweating through every pore.

In bed that night Janine snuggled up to him, clearly tired and a little bit drunk.

"Evelyn was right; you are brave George."

George held her tenderly in his arms and drifted off to sleep vaguely wondering how he had impressed so many women so easily.

<u>Chapter Six: The Truth hits home</u>

"What knife throwing act?" George asked at breakfast the next day.

Janine was still a bit hung-over but had a clear recollection of what had been discussed.

"You didn't have that much to drink last night. Lola's knife throwing act; you agreed to take part."

This was news to George. A vague recollection of agreeing to something and being praised by all concerned crept back into his brain.

"Oh yes, that," he said unconvincingly. "Now that I think about it though, I can't really throw knives, so it would be too dangerous for Lola."

"Didn't you listen to anything we said last night?" continued Janine. "You don't have to worry about that, remember? She'll be throwing knives at you!"

The morning had started badly for George and appeared to be falling away. He had been in the process of spreading marmalade onto a piece of toast as Janine detailed his commitment from the night before. He watched in a dream as the marmalade slipped from his knife onto the tablecloth. As Janine spoke, George realised why the girls had been so impressed by his bravery and why Janine had paused when he had agreed. He scraped the marmalade off the table and spread it on his toast. As far as he could make out he had agreed to be the target for Lola as she tried to gain work as a circus knife-thrower, having never worked as such before. Her previous job in that field hadn't worked out, was all he knew. He looked at Janine out of the corner of his eye. She appeared to be fine with this arrangement. It also seemed to be part of her plan to move Lola on from their house. Reluctant as he was to rule out any more naked flamenco, he was keen to return to a more relaxed and, in some ways, boring existence. Overall then, it was fine by him.

"That'll be okay then," he confirmed as he ate his toast.

Chapter Seven: Rehearsals

Janine insisted on coming along to the first rehearsal that Lola had arranged with George. Partly this was because the revolving wheel being used was still in the basement of Lola's dominatrix friend in Edinburgh. Mainly it was because Janine wanted to make sure that Lola was only interested in George as a target for her knives. Also she was concerned about Lola's claim of accuracy.

Thus the three of them travelled through to Edinburgh and arrived at a surprisingly fashionable address one Monday morning when they had been assured they would have a quiet morning to use the facilities. Lola's friend appeared at the door and let them in on her way to work as a University librarian, insisting that they were out by one o'clock as her flexi hours had allowed her to meet with a client for an hour's fun before the afternoon part of her shift.

Janine and George were fascinated by what they found in the basement but Lola quickly went into professional mode, to the point of changing into a sequined leotard before the session began. As before, her lack of modesty meant she did this in full view of her hosts but with Janine there, George averted his eyes.

"Let's give it a whirl," said Lola with a laugh and spun the wheel.

George felt a little bit queasy but smiled as the details were discussed. Lola calmed down and agreed to demonstrate her silky skills before George risked life and limb. This was largely at Janine's insistence.

George and Janine stood well back where they could get a good view and watched Lola, looking the part in her sequined leotard and feather headdress. She focused on the wheel, which was around six feet in diameter and no longer spinning. She picked up a pile of 12 throwing knives with sparkling purple handles and took aim. Around the wheel there were ten stars painted around the edge and Lola threw a knife neatly into the centre of each. The final two she threw into the centre of the wheel with expert aim and turned, taking a bow from the genuinely impressed audience. Her aim was very accurate and her confidence reassuring to both George and Janine.

After a brief discussion George put on an overly large frock coat and top hat and took hold of the knives which he found were actually quite heavy. Following the instruction he walked towards the wheel with a sense of purpose, bowed and waved the knives in a confident manner. As Lola met up with George, centre stage, they exchanged a look and he handed the knives over to her.

With an exaggerated expression they swapped roles and George stood in front of the wheel with Lola staring at the knives in disbelief. Then without a word of warning Lola threw the knives into the stars on the wheel and placed the final ones between George's legs.

"Ta da!" she said as she finished and Janine clapped enthusiastically, relieved that George was unscathed.

George was initially less enthusiastic, but as he checked for injury and realised there was none, he too clapped, but more in relief than praise. After a pause Lola suggested she try the finale and Janine and George agreed with an element of reservation after exchanging glances. Lola and Janine secured George to the wheel and then Janine placed a blindfold over Lola's eyes. Lola spun the wheel and slowly took twelve exaggerated paces away from it. She turned back towards the rotating George and threw the knives one by one in a slow and deliberate manner. Again the final two were placed accurately between George's legs.

Lola removed the blindfold cautiously and looked at the wheel. A look of relief spread over her face as she confirmed the knives were all safely embedded in the wheel and not George. Janine hoped that the look of relief was part of the act but was not one hundred per cent convinced. The two women smiled and clapped and gave each other a brief hug. George continued to revolve in the background with his eyes shut.

"Well done Lola," enthused Janine. "You are deadly with those things; or not, as the case may be. Either way you hit the spot every time."

"I told you I could do it. Wait till the agent sees the act. Well done, George, but try and keep your eyes open next time."

"Let me off," wailed George, who was promptly sick as soon as his hands and legs were freed.

"The wheel takes a bit of getting used to," advised Lola. "Best not to eat too much before a performance next time. Let's have another run through."

George turned pale at the thought and Janine stepped in quickly, seeing his discomfort.

"Probably best without the finale; just the knives."

George found this only slightly less worrying as it was partly being a target that had made him ill with nerves rather than simply the motion of the wheel. Nevertheless, he went through a further rehearsal, actually quite enjoying the play-acting part. Once all the knives were safely in the wheel again, he and Lola took a bow with Janine clapping enthusiastically from the side.

Chapter Eight: Benny Goldflab, Special Agent

Benny Goldflab had failed to make it big as a stand-up Jewish comic in London during the 70s and 80s. Had he been born in an earlier era he would have failed to make it big as a stand-up Jewish comic during the 30s and 40s, when they at least had a fighting chance. He had in fact since failed to make it big in anything else. To survive, however, he had diversified into managing other, better, acts which he realised had a future. None of them made it big either but he gathered enough desperate souls under his wing for them all to earn a crust. He became especially good at finding work for the more unusual acts other agents and managers wouldn't touch. Benny liked to think that he specialised in the exotic by choice, but he needed clients if he was to be a manager.

His client list had everything from a sword swallower to a one legged tightrope walker who had a habit of falling off the wire. There were a particularly large proportion of circus acts without circuses and Benny had managed to find almost all of them work from time to time. He had a reputation amongst such acts of never turning them down. He would hold quarterly auditions for those seeking his services in a warehouse on the outskirts of the city and these were universally known as Benny's Big Tops. As a result of his rather unorthodox client base, he was known in the industry as The Special Agent. Benny liked the nickname and even had cards printed with 'Benny Goldflab – Special Agent' on them. He never actually handed them out to anyone other than friends and family, but he liked having them in his desk to look at from time to time.

Lola had met Benny at a party in London and he had never forgotten her. She had never forgotten his promise that he could find regular work for anyone. Beyond that he meant nothing to her. For Benny it was love and lust at first sight. Despite a wife and three children, Benny would have dropped everything and followed her to the ends of the earth. This was due to a combination of Lola's natural beauty, her alluring physical poise and vitality and Benny's complete disinterest in his wife Rachel.

Had Lola known exactly how smitten Benny would become, she might have avoided brushing her hand against the front of his trousers and winking as she said goodbye and left the party. To her it was her usual way of ensuring that men who might later prove useful to her remembered her name at least. Benny remembered far more than that as he regularly stared at the photographs in Lola's file which she had forwarded to his office. Most had her dressed in skimpy costumes with feather headdresses in place but the one which he found most difficult to put down showed her in a flamenco dress swirling with her hands in the air. He had never seen such beauty, he thought, certainly never in his matrimonial home. The single caress of Lola's hand across his crotch had placed him under a spell which could not be broken. He was not the only such victim Lola had left in her wake, but few suffered as badly as Benny.

Benny spent days staring at his phone hoping Lola would call after the party and moped home each night in abject disappointment when she didn't. Eventually he plucked up the courage to phone her, not to ask her out or anything - his courage was quite limited - just to hear her voice. As an excuse, he told her that it was his habit to phone all his clients on a regular basis and make sure they were in good health and available for work. If Benny had actually done this his meagre profits would have been more than used up in phone calls.

Lola was both surprised and pleased to hear his voice on the phone but disappointed when she realised he was not calling with the offer of work. She perked up when he assured her that he would find her plenty before suggesting she came round to his office one day to talk through all the skills she had to offer; she needn't wait for the next of Benny's Big Tops. Lola had heard that one before but felt, correctly, that she could handle Benny and would be quite safe.

Benny put the receiver of his phone back on its old fashioned cradle and sighed a deep sigh of satisfaction. Lola Cortez was coming to his office in two days' time to run through her CV and to demonstrate her circus and dancing skills: a visit which would include her dancing the flamenco in her swirling red dress. That gave Benny just under 48 hours to make himself irresistible to a beautiful woman almost half his age. A tall order on the face of it, but he had a secret weapon: he was a personal friend of Mystero the Stage Magician, who knew everything there was to know about women. Not only could Mystero saw them in half and put them back together, but he could do the same with their hearts. He was a serial philanderer of the first order and had a phonebook with hundreds of women's numbers in it, many the young mothers of children whose birthday parties he had entertained.

Benny was blinded to the fact that Mystero was 10 years younger, tall and handsome with a strong but not overly muscled physique. Instead he focused on the few similarities: both had a moustache, both were in show business. That was it really.

Benny phoned Mystero at his flat in Milton Keynes.

"Hi buddy, Benny here, how's tricks?"

"All good thanks. You?"

"Nicely, nicely," replied Benny, quoting his favourite character from Guys and Dolls.

"You able to talk at the moment?"

"Sure," said Mystero, whose real name was Kevin Smith.

"I need your help, big time," said Benny.

"Anything my friend, just name it."

The two men had become unlikely friends, having entered into a business relationship by accident. Kevin had been performing at a bar mitzvah which Benny had been at with his wife and their first child. His act was dreadful, but Benny saw the possibilities, and approached Kevin, who at the time appeared as The Amazing Kevin Smith, with the suggestion of becoming his agent and advisor. Kevin had been struggling for work for good reasons but was determined to succeed in the world of stage magicians. An intensive period of mentoring followed, at the end of which, Mystero the Magician emerged, butterfly-like, with a new costumes and a much improved act. He gained a few bookings from Benny straight away and word spread around the fashionable mums of Golders Green and further afield about the handsome young children's entertainer, whose big thing was magic.

Benny was pleased to have an act on his books who gained regular work. Kevin was delighted to get regular bookings from Benny and soon realised there could be other perks from his trade. As a result the two became firm friends and Benny loved to hear details of Kevin's latest exploits.

"I have met this woman and I need your help," began Benny.

"I see, you old rogue," said Kevin.

"No, no, it's nothing like that," protested Benny before adding after due consideration, "I suppose actually, it is exactly like that. I really need to impress her and I only have 48 hours to get ready."

"I am a magician, Benny boy, but even I have limits! Just kidding, I owe you a lot. Take down the address of my London barber and head over there now. Say I sent you and that he is to work his magic: trust me; he could put my act to shame. Then get back to your office. I'll be there on the next train."

Benny wrote down the name and address of what looked and sounded like an expensive barber's and put his answer machine setting to 'on'. If anyone could give him a chance with Lola it was The Amazing Kevin Smith.

Chapter Nine: Lola's Audition

Benny sat in his office feeling slightly uncomfortable in the new clothes he had bought with Kevin the day before, and with the tidiest hair he had had in years. Overall though, he felt more comfortable at the prospect of interviewing Lola than he had when they had spoken at first on the phone. Kevin had given him a whole load of sound advice regarding women and he was running through it in his head whilst simultaneously reading the bullet points from the memory cards he had made up in order to leave nothing to chance.

His confidence however evaporated when Lola knocked at his office door and let herself in, pulling a flight case behind her.

"Benny darling, how are you," Lola gushed more through habit than genuine concern for his well-being. "There's something different about you too," she added, not quite sure what it was.

Benny nearly tripped as he stood up to take her hand and welcome her to his office. He managed to mumble something about getting a haircut before offering Lola a cup of tea.

"No thank you, Benny. I struggle to get into my costume as it is without a full bladder as well."

It was hardly romantic banter but Benny didn't mind. He had Lola in his office and she could have discussed anything she wanted to, just as long as he could drink in her beauty. He stared enraptured as she discussed the queue for the bus and the puddles which threatened her feet, more used as they were to sunnier climes. Her tales of toast for breakfast and running out of marmalade had him on the edge of his seat.

Eventually after a prolonged silence he felt obliged to discuss work.

"You told me you were a dancer and knife thrower?"

"Yes, although they are separate skills. I never combine the two for safety reasons."

There was a pause before Lola burst out laughing at her wit. Dutifully, Benny joined in, just a little too enthusiastically.

"I suppose you would like me to demonstrate? I thought the dancing might be safest. The knives might damage your décor."

"Of course," agreed Benny, waiting to see if he should again laugh but this time not getting a cue.

He was about to suggest Lola made use of his toilet for changing when she stood up, placed her raincoat over her chair and wriggled out of the dress she wore beneath it. Benny was spell bound. He was sure that nobody could wriggle quite like Lola could. She was wearing nothing underneath and casually reached into her flight case and took out the flamenco dress Benny had so admired in her photograph. Again he watched her wriggle, but this time into the dress. It was indeed a bit tight on her contours but no red blooded man would ever have complained. Once her dress had been smoothed down, Lola reached into the case again and brought out a small CD player. She put on some music and began to dance in time to the beat. She had clearly studied flamenco dancing and added a pair of maracas to the ensemble for the second tune.

After ten minutes or so Lola stopped and looked up at Benny.

"What do you think? Can you find me work?"

Benny nodded, unable to say a word for fear of mumbling incoherently.

"I've left the knives at home, but you might want to check out the costume for that act while I'm here."

Again Benny managed to nod but achieved nothing else. He watched transfixed as Lola began wriggling out of the dress and then into a sequinned leotard and feather headband.

"The big gag is that I appear with an old duffer who looks like every other knife thrower in the world. The audience assume I'm the token crumpet who gets the knives thrown at them. Then I take the knives from him and he lines up at the target while I throw the knives. Gasps all round and applause when they realise I can really throw them, even blind-folded."

Benny was nodding now, almost uncontrollably but managed to mumble, "Even blind-folded."

"What do you think Benny? It's brilliant isn't it?"

Benny had to agree it was a new twist on an old act. If Lola could somehow work a bit of flamenco dancing into the act there was something for most audiences. If she changed in front of them there was something for everyone.

"I like it," he managed to say with all sincerity. "I will check all my bookings and see what we can start you off with. Who does the straight man bit?"

"Oh, there are a few old friends I can rope in when I need to," Lola lied so confidently that Benny didn't give it another thought "I'd better just change back into my normal clothes before I go outside. I wouldn't get far in this get-up."

Benny again nodded before mumbling, "Yes, best change."

Once Lola had wriggled, changed and left, Benny sat back in his chair, a tortured man. He knew that, for better or worse, for richer or poorer, in sickness and in health his life would never be the same again. He would never be the same again. He had sampled the smallest taste of ambrosia and could never return to bagels.

Chapter Ten: Grand Pacific hotel

The incongruously named Grand Pacific Hotel stood on the South side of one of the city centre squares in Edinburgh's New Town. It loomed over the grassed gardens in the middle of what was now essentially a massive roundabout, like a huge architectural cake. It had been built in the days of wealthy Victorian train travel and had moved down the food chain of accommodation ever since. Originally commissioned as The Czarina Grand Hotel it had changed names with owners until a Californian Group had briefly acquired it and a name finally stuck. This slide might have continued until it was inevitably converted into flats, if it had not been spotted by an international Hotel Group who saw in it a strategic real estate investment. They added it to their worldwide collection of city centre destinations and refurbished it accordingly. All rooms were upgraded to a high standard in the décor they boasted was by a famous French designer. Staff were replaced or intensively trained in the corporate standards and a luxury pool, gym and spa centre installed in the basement. The company spent a fortune on the place and wanted to recoup it. Their business model was quite simple: keep the place full. As a result any organisation which could fill ten or more rooms was welcomed with generous discounts. If one could fill the whole hotel for more than one night they were welcomed with open arms by the management and given rooms at a fraction of the regular price.

The British Society of Gentlemen's Gentlemen held a lavish convention every second year. It was lavish for two reasons: firstly, the modern butler was generally a very well paid individual with no accommodation expenses; and secondly, their employers were expected to pay the cost of attending. There was an element of competitive consumption amongst some of the employers, especially the Americans who employed British (pronounced English) butlers. Some butlers had their reservations about crossing the pond without a British employer in tow but it was an open secret that Americans would pay the best rates. One butler was rumoured to be paid almost $250,000 per year to attend to the needs of a rap star based in Hollywood.

During the daytime of each event there were presentations on all aspects of the butler's trade: everything from traditional silver polishing to the more modern requirements of security for their employers. All these things were big business nowadays and companies paid well to have a good pitch in the main exhibition hall.

On the first evening there was always a dinner accompanied by a floor show. The show was organised by the hotel hosting the event and each would try to outdo the event hosted by its predecessor. Over the years the delegates had witnessed everything from pantomime, vaudeville and burlesque, to opera, ballet, variety and even dancing on ice.

Each hotel would try to keep the arrangements a secret until the night itself and anticipation would build up as rumours circulated in a mood of boyish good humour.

The second evening took the form of a formal dinner where, for once, the heads of so many large households were waited on by staff rather than the other way round. It was always known as the Butler's Ball although there was no formal dancing or partners involved. The event was an opportunity for the normally staid butlers to let their hair down, whether they had any left or not. Drink flowed throughout the night and tales were never told outwith school. What happened at the Butlers Ball stayed at the Butlers' Ball. Professional speakers would be hired to entertain after dinner and the proceedings were introduced and controlled by the Master of The British Society of Gentlemen's Gentlemen. This office was not filled by a butler; that would never do. Instead, the post for life was held by a member of the British aristocracy, elected by ballot on the death or resignation through ill health of each incumbent. As well as being a Baronet or better, the Master had also to be a player of the highest order, somebody who could be relied upon to keep the whole event fun; boisterous but out of the papers. The present Master was all of those things and much more. Lord Strathbole was the 9th of his line and had been a wild man in his youth. A rake of the first order, he and his friends had made the Bullingdon club look like a pack of Brownies at church camp, while he was at Oxford. He had cut a swathe through the young ladies of the aristocracy, along with some of their mothers, and, in one well reported episode, the grandmother of one of his friends. Paternity suits had followed him around the world like bees round a honeycomb. His family solicitors had had to work like Trojans to preserve the family fortunes during these formative years. Fortunately for Lord Strathbole and unfortunately for the single mothers involved, his philandering days all preceded both fully equal rights and the Child Support Agency.

When the Butler's Ball was in the early planning stages, one of the management staff suggested a circus theme and further helped by producing the contact details of Benny Goldflab who specialised in such acts. The planning committee included occasional input from Lord Strathbole, who thought it a splendid idea, and Benny was tasked to produce amazing acts which could all be performed in the confines of a hotel ballroom. The only condition was that the acts should be sensational and include live lions. Benny struggled with this, but knew enough people to ask around and organise what was required. The booking allowed him to provide work for a number of his clients and in particular it offered him the opportunity to give Lola her first booking. He suggested to her that for this performance she played safe and used somebody she had used before. Lola was thrilled when she got Benny's call, and knew just the man for the job.

<u>Chapter Eleven: Friends in Low Places</u>

Lord Strathbole had a large estate in Perthshire as well as a townhouse in London and a spacious pied-à-terre in Edinburgh. All of these things had been inherited and saved during his wild youth along with sufficient capital to survive well until a wealthy maiden aunt died in the year 2000. Lord Strathbole, as the only living relative, had inherited her substantial fortune and thereafter increased his style of living accordingly. He had got married quite late in life to a stunning society belle and they had had one child together, a boy called Simon Peter, reflecting his mother's religious inclinations rather than his father's inclinations which had nothing to do with religion. Feeling that he had done his duty by both his wife and his ancestors, Lord Strathbole, or Hamish to his close friends, returned to his former life of carousing and wild living, leaving his wife to raise Simon. She was, of course, greatly aided in this task by a household of servants in Perthshire and London (she never stayed in her husband's house in Edinburgh), many of whom had been with the family for years, along with a few who had been transferred like footballers from her own family home when she married.

All the staff were regularly briefed on the need for discretion and reminded by the family lawyer of the confidentiality agreements which they had signed. As a result, little of note escaped the confines of the households and into the papers via staff members past or present. Within the staff, however, was a small group who were required to keep secrets not only from the press but also from other members of the Strathbole family. For Lady Fiona Strathbole that was limited to two of the staff who had transferred with her. For Lord Strathbole that meant his valet, the butler, the chauffeur and Billy Winkman who worked in the Perthshire stables.

Billy Winkman was originally from darkest Dundee and would no doubt have come to a sticky end were it not for the fact that he had a special affinity with horses. This had come to light working at weekends with his uncle who was employed at a local equitation centre. Billy's uncle had no great gift with horses and spent most of his working day mucking out the stables, then selling the manure to gardeners nearby.

Billy loved escaping from the streets of Dundee to the countryside with his uncle and quickly established himself at the centre as someone who could handle any horse there and also calm them down when they got unsettled. He was not a horse whisperer as such; more of a horse curser, going by his foul language, but there was something in the rapport he could establish with them that made him stand out from the other staff.

As time passed and he failed to sprout beyond the five foot four inch mark he headed naturally towards a career as a jockey. He rode several winners in his first season, all of them rank outsiders. Punters, trainers and owners alike took note of Billy Winkman and his winning ways. A successful future beckoned but as with most of his family, Billy managed to snatch defeat from the jaws of victory.

Billy's abilities may have been in working with horses but his passion was boxing. He had trained for the ring from an early age and never missed a training session. Unfortunately for him his enthusiasm was never matched by his abilities, and he slowly built up a cabinet full of second prizes. All the tools of the boxer's trade were there; a powerful right hook, a vicious left jab and a chin that could take a punch like few others. Billy just couldn't bring them to bear at the right moment of his fights. He would loose off a right when it was well covered by his opponent, or left when there was nobody there to connect with. He could also bob and weave his way onto the slowest of punches. The result was an amateur career where he was never knocked out but instead was knocked about the ring by even the rawest of novices.

Billy was undeterred, convinced he had a glittering future in boxing which would eclipse his career riding horses and so he turned professional. Maybe he was right; or maybe he had taken one too many on the chin to see his boxing abilities for what they were. Whatever the truth of the matter, both careers came to a crashing end after yet another loss, this time to Eddie 'the Hurricane' McIntyre from Glasgow. As usual Billy had lacked the good sense to fall down and the judges were forced to witness another beating before Eddie was declared the winner in a unanimous decision. Billy felt he had been robbed, as did the crowd who had paid good money to watch. He threw on his clothes without showering, jumped into his car and drove to his local pub. There he drowned his sorrows with friends - all prepared to agree the decision had been flawed in return for free drink.

After getting his blood alcohol level close to five times the legal limit, he left the bar and jumped into his car, intent on driving to Glasgow for a rematch with 'the Hurricane'. He did surprisingly well to reach the final junction where Riverside Avenue meets the A90 south heading towards Glasgow, before he lost control and ended up perched on the roundabout itself. Someone stopped and called the emergency services before retreating to their car in the face of threats from Billy.

The ambulance arrived shortly before the police, and the paramedics, sensing Billy's mood, waited to see who would be their casualty for the run back to Nine Wells hospital. Billy appeared unhurt but was obviously very drunk. The police officers tried to calm him down in order to arrest him for drink driving but he was having none of it. When the female officer stepped forward and invited him to the ambulance to get checked out, Billy mistook it for the start of another boxing match and put her down in the first. Her colleague weighed in against Billy in fury, seeking vengeance for his injured partner. For once in Billy's life all his skills came together and he could not put a fist wrong. Although he fought at bantamweight and was giving away a lot of pounds to everyone on the roundabout, including the female PC, he quickly floored the second policeman with a brilliant flurry of jabs before taking out both paramedics. Had it not been for a local rugby team returning to Perth by coach passing a few minutes later, Billy might have worked his way through the population of Dundee before sobering up. Two prop forwards brought him down and held him there until police reinforcements arrived, one getting a black eye for his troubles.

By the time Billy woke up the following day he had been charged with a variety of violent offences, all shaded up to more serious levels on account of his boxing licence. A well-meaning legal aid-funded lawyer advised Billy to plead guilty to lesser charges on the grounds of diminished responsibility, but the jury were having none of it. In a lengthy summing up, the judge took account of everything he could find which worked against Billy, including a string of juvenile offences. In particular he majored on the fact that the female paramedic, a grandmother of fifty three, was unlikely to return to work. He was less sympathetic regarding the two police officers who had filled in criminal injuries paperwork almost before they reached the hospital. Reading between the lines, he seemed to believe Billy was a nasty piece of work and a danger to the public, a public who deserved a long break from him. In sentencing him to six years he warned Billy to use the time inside to reflect on the error of his ways.

When Billy was finally released, having demonstrated no good behaviour to shorten his sentence, he found himself unemployable in either of his previous professions. His boxing career was finished stone dead, despite the promise he had shown on the roundabout, and none of his previous racing contacts wanted to take a chance with him, even allowing for his ability handling horses and his undoubted riding talent.

Life seemed to have removed any possibilities of a future for Billy until he happened to bump into that well-known patron of the turf, Lord Strathbole. They met by chance at a race meeting in Hamilton, his Lordship there to watch one of his horses finish sixth and Billy hopeful of bumping into someone who might offer him a job. As

Billy walked round the paddock he failed to connect with any previous business associates and had started to give up hope when he happened to lean on the rails beside Lord Strathbole. His Lordship was boasting about his horse's chances in the 'Badger Windscreen Replacement Hurdles' to the young lady on his arm, who was not his wife. Billy listened to a stream of compliments for 'Gadgie's Lad' before he could stand it no longer and chipped in: "Not a fucking chance."

Lord Strathbole was about to walk away whilst eyeing daggers at Billy when he recognised him as a figure who had ridden a few winners in the past. Keen to take any advantage available, he turned to Billy and enquired why Gadgie's Lad might not win.

Billy eyed him up and down before summing up his opinion.

"It's no walking right. It's been spooked."

"Really," said Lord Strathbole. "How can you tell?"

Billy stared at his lordship without reverence or disdain before adding: "Just the way he walks. And the way the Irish jockeys are betting."

Hamish was interested, knowing full well his own horse had little chance of romping home as an outsider.

"Who would you put your money on then?" he asked Billy.

"Well, I don't have any money, but if I were you, I would put my money on No 10. It has the look of a winner to me, not that I have any money, mind."

"I couldn't possibly bet against my own horse; that would be quite wrong."

"A pity," said Billy. "There's more chance of the pope giving birth to black twins than that donkey of yours winning today."

Lord Strathbole had to agree, looking at the rest of the card, but he couldn't be seen to bet against his own horse, donkey or not.

"If you had some of my money for instance, with no strings attached as it were, you could bet how you saw fit."

"I could, but why would I?" replied Billy.

"Well, apart from splitting any winnings 50/50 there might be some work in it for you, if you're interested. I remember you winning a few races in the past, and I made a bob or two before your untimely incarceration."

Billy was very interested and became more so when Lord Strathbole placed a wad of £500 into his hand and encouraged him to go with his gut instincts.

Twenty five minutes later Billy was collecting £3500 from an on-course bookie, having watched number ten beat the opposition at a canter. As Lord Strathbole had anticipated, Billy now experienced a moment of indecision. Should he do a runner with the money or hand it over to his Lordship and hope for more of the same? It was a very difficult decision to make. On the one hand he had more raw cash in his possession at that moment than he had ever had before. If he legged it with the money, his Lordship was unlikely to take action, as to do so would make it known to all concerned that he had placed his money on a rival's horse - something which would have threatened his racing licence. On the other hand, trust had been placed in Billy for the first time in years, and by somebody who even remembered his glory days riding winners. If he took the money back he had been promised half the winnings. That was still a lot of money. It was a dilemma right enough. In the end Billy decided honesty might just be the best policy and returned to the enclosure to seek out Lord Strathbole.

When Hamish saw Billy Winkman return he was both pleased and surprised. He had half expected that he would never see his money again, but instead the battered little man had returned with several thousand pounds of winnings.

"Keep it this time round," he told an equally surprised Billy. "I suspect we may be able to do more business. What are you up to these days, anyway?"

Billy was about to make up a story of a relatively happy existence when he stopped and gave in to the mutual spirit of honesty.

"I've been struggling a bit, your Lordship, with all that happened. I'm living in a transition hostel looking for work."

"You're not working with horses then?" asked Strathbole with genuine interest.

"Not many trainers want anything to do with me. My CV has a bit of a gap, " said Billy in a mock formal accent.

"What a shame. I heard several people say you were the best groom in the business, not to mention your riding skills."

"I was good sir, that's true, but I'll never get my licence back now. Not after what I did to my cell mate in Saughton."

"Really?" said Hamish, warming to Billy. "Why don't you come and work for me with my horses in Perthshire?"

"I'd need to square it with my probation officer and the judge, but sounds good. In fact, thank you, sir, I'd be delighted to have the chance."

"I'll speak to your judge, I'm sure I'll know him. Of course there might be a few other jobs for you to do from time to time. No names no pack drill for now, but I rather think this could be the beginning of a beautiful friendship, as it were."

With that the two men shook hands, and one week later Billy moved into a cottage beside the stables at Strathbole Castle, much to the consternation of the staff there, and the Factor in particular. Despite their reservations though, everyone had to admit that his lordship's horses started to perform far better when racing than they had ever done before. Along with a few bargain purchases made by his lordship with Billy in tow, the reputation of the stables rose significantly thereafter.

For his part, Billy was delighted to be working with horses again. It was the thing he knew he was best at, and a quiet life in the grounds of the castle suited him just fine. As an occasional bit of excitement he would travel out with his Lordship, usually to Edinburgh where he could anonymously source a variety of items, substances or individuals for his lordship's pleasure. As a rare treat he would also have to lie in wait with a baseball bat or similar to avenge an insult inflicted on his new boss.

Over all, as far as it went for an ex–con, life was surprisingly good.

Chapter Twelve: Meanwhile Back at the Ranch

One element of George's life which hadn't changed when Janine moved in was his regular, if unimpressive, appearances at the dart board in The Ranch public house. The old gang were all there and George found that his standing had rising as a result of his recent exploits against Frankie Cook and his liaison with former barmaid Janine in particular. Either way he was glad to have maintained the stability of his friendships at the dart board.

"So are they all gay?" asked Old Jock having missed the point as usual.

The rest of the group stared at him for a moment before Willie Taylor set matters straight as always.

"No. 'Gentleman's gentleman' means Butler. They're all butlers."

"Why no just say that then?" responded Old Jock.

"It's an ancient society," added George. "Some of them are almost aristocracy themselves. Besides, they can earn more if they use the old fashioned terminology."

"So this Lola bird throws knives at you?" enquired Willie, genuinely intrigued.

"Aye, but she never misses. She could hit a midge's willy at fifty feet," confirmed George.

Old Jock tried to picture a midge's willy close up, never mind fifty feet away, and realised how impressive a feat that would be.

"Should you be taking these risks at your age?" asked young Gordon Beaton, as ever thinking about the age issues and for once not being admonished by the others.

"The wheel spinning makes me sick but otherwise I'm as safe as houses," countered George.

"What if she has an off day or it's her time of the month or something?" enquired Ray Lindsay with an air of genuine concern.

"Don't talk shit," said Gordon's girlfriend Jenny who had recently taken to playing darts, much to everyone's surprise and annoyance. "We don't become disabled once a month. Good on her for challenging female stereotypes."

"It's not a gender issue," said Willie in his customary moderate tone. "We're concerned at anyone throwing knives at George, even if he is getting paid for it."

"It's just till she finds someone from the industry," said George. Looking round he saw no likely volunteers and realised he was far away from Lola's circus crowd. "Once she has made a name for herself I'm off the hook and she can travel the world with her act."

"Assuming she doesn't make a name for herself by sticking a knife in someone and going to jail first," said Jock before returning to the dart board and taking his turn.

The others tried not to think that Jock was being prophetic for the first time in his life but acknowledged that they had some concerns none the less.

Chapter Thirteen: Eric Ramsay

Eric Ramsay had been born into private service in the way that slaves were once born into slavery. His parents were both in service to a Duke at the time, and it was all he had ever known. He grew up learning the requirements of the trade by osmosis as he watched his mother and father go about their duties and eventually rise to the positions of Butler and Housekeeper in the Duke's grand country house. By the time he was sixteen he was tall enough to fit his father's old livery, with a bit of adjustment at the waist by his mother, and thereafter regularly worked at the large functions or deputised for other staff members. Eventually this included his father when he had days off or was ill, both of which were rare.

The main difference between slavery and service was that Eric loved it. He loved the grandeur of the house where he lived and grew up, almost friends with the Duke's children who were roughly the same age. As youngsters they would roam the grounds during the summer holidays, building dens, making bows and arrows and getting filthy with the same dirt. When they returned each evening they were equals in the face of the bath and complaints from both Eric's mother and the governess, Nanny Sykes. Once cleaned and dressed, though, they parted for very different evenings with their families, a separation which grew with age, just like the boys themselves.

By the time the Duke's brood went to their Oxbridge destinies, Eric was a full time employee in the household and their paths rarely crossed outwith the formality of the castle's main rooms. Eric didn't mind. He knew his place and saw the development as quite natural. If anything he felt privileged to have spent so much time with the boys and their sister, bearing in mind the difference in their station. After all, young Ralph would one day become the ninth Duke. Eric's best hope was to rise to be his butler.

Eric grew into a good looking young man who attracted the casual gaze of many of the young girls on the staff and many of the young ladies who came to stay at the castle. Along with his looks he attracted attention by virtue of the family trait whereby his eyebrows were black from the age of seventeen while his hair was a rich mane of golden locks. His father and grandfather had been similarly afflicted until their hair and eyebrows all turned grey and finally matched. At first the interest was only casual on both sides but finally one visitor to the castle took a shine to young Eric and found a reason for him to bring a glass of mineral water to her bedroom around midnight on her second night there. Eric sneaked back to his own room around three in the morning, a little confused but rather happy. From that point onwards he cut a swathe through the female staff at the castle and was called upon to provide more than just an occasional glass of mineral water for some of the ladies visiting the Duke and Duchess.

His parents were aware of some of his affairs below stairs but remained blissfully unaware of those above. When he was in his mid-twenties however, there was something of a scandal involving a recently widowed society lady in her forties. No details leaked to the press but it was an open secret in the staff quarters of the castle that the Duke had sneaked into the lady's room hoping to comfort her only to find the butler's son had beaten him to it. Outrage ensued all round, and Eric quietly left the Duke's service and took up the position of butler with a school-friend of the Duke's, Lord Strathbole.

Eric settled into the role there as if raised to the task, which indeed he had been. He stayed in Lord Strathbole's employ for over ten years until, out of the blue he moved to Europe to work for a German count, for no apparent reason that anyone could make out. There he had remained, avoiding Britain the rest of the time as far as any of his former colleagues was concerned.

This had been the pattern of his life until his final, fateful return to the UK.

Chapter Fourteen: Lady Strathbole's problem

The years since her marriage had not been kind to Lady Fiona Strathbole, or, more accurately, Lord Strathbole had not been kind to her, and this had taken its toll in more ways than one. It became clear shortly after the wedding (about three hours or so to be exact) that Hamish had no intentions of settling down to a quiet life of marital bliss. Although they enjoyed some semblance of married life and shared the matrimonial bed from time to time, it was clear that Lord Strathbole regarded it as a marriage for his convenience only. For her part Fiona was expected to run the domestic matters of Strathbole Castle and the London home and to be available for her husband as required. Beyond that she was left to her own devices. Having expected to spend her time with Hamish, entertaining, travelling or discussing the business of running the estate, she was disappointed to be allocated no more than a bit part in her husband's life.

As a result she tried to throw herself into the activities of the local Perthshire community or London society, only occasionally accompanied by her husband. London offered her the chance to keep in touch with many of her old friends, but she was aware that they knew of her time alone and the rumours of Hamish's extra marital activities, and she felt embarrassed. In Perthshire though, she found herself able to relax and be her old humorous and sociable self again, nowhere more so than at the Castle, surrounded by an attendant staff and beautiful grounds. Her own staff who came with her when she married were very sympathetic to her plight from the off, but she soon realised that the existing staff at the castle appeared to feel sorry for her too. The two forces of London embarrassment and Perthshire comfort, slowly but surely resulted in her withdrawal from the South and almost permanent residence in the North. This suited Hamish fine, as did her refusal to accompany him to his townhouse in Edinburgh. After a few years of marriage it was as if the castle had always been her home and Hamish was the incomer. His absences became welcome rather than just bearable, and she could be cheerful for days in the rooms and gardens of the stately home.

Her mother had brought her up with the stiffest of upper lips and schooled her from an early age to hide her feelings from the staff at all costs - partly, as she admitted, because their lives were almost certainly worse than hers, no matter how low she ever felt. If you must show your feelings to any of the staff it must only be to the butler, so that he can ensure the necessary support from the other staff; that was his job after all. No doubt Lady Isabella had been picturing the elderly retainers from her own household over the years, seeing them as almost family and a safe, fatherly if not grandfatherly, figure of support. Her advice had not been designed to deal with young Eric Ramsay's rise to the position of butler at such an early and attractive stage of his life.

Her mother's advice came back to Lady Fiona on the rare occasions when she felt low, needed support and her own maids wouldn't do. "A last resort shoulder to cry on," her mother had called old Chalmers the family butler, no doubt thinking of funerals and the like. Young Eric's broad young shoulders looked far more inviting to stain with tears and Lady Fiona found herself comforted by him one day after a row on the telephone with her husband who was in Edinburgh.

It was only a brief moment of contact in her study after she had slammed the phone down and burst into tears. Eric had been very kind and professional, and had assured Lady Fiona that he would ensure the staff kept their distance for the rest of the morning until she had regained her composure. He had instinctively tilted her head on to his shoulder as she sobbed. His hand had rested on her hair and then he had stroked it whispering: "There, there, Madam. Don't upset yourself."

Nothing more; just a human act of kindness, but one which had been so lacking in her life to date that she remembered the feeling of security it had provided for the rest of the day. As she recovered her spirits she felt slightly embarrassed by her earlier behaviour, and had asked Eric to meet her in the drawing room after dinner in order to apologise. She promised herself afterwards that that had been all she had wanted to do. When Eric arrived though, immaculately turned out, young and strong, she had weakened. She started to apologise about the tears and using his shoulder to cry on. Her attempt at making a joke of the whole thing failed, her words stuttered and refused to come out in any coherent order. She felt the tears returning and finally simply whispered: "Hold me again please, Eric."

"Certainly Madam," said Eric who had dismissed all the other staff from the main rooms of the castle to ensure her ladyship was given privacy and peace. He promised himself afterwards that that had been all he had wanted to do.

Chapter Fifteen: His Lordship's Vengeance

Rumours of impropriety at the castle eventually reached Lord Strathbole in London through the usual channel, that is to say, via his chauffeur. Long hours on the road together, often to meet ladies who were not Her Ladyship, had produced a strong bond between Hamish and James. During a conversation when James had heard a comment from the housekeeper at the castle regarding the possibility of a rather close friendship developing between Lady Fiona and Eric the Butler, he had felt obliged to tell his lordship. Despite his own conduct, Hamish was livid and cancelled all meetings, business or pleasure for the next two weeks and headed home.

At the castle he confronted his wife who broke down and admitted to having an affair with the butler. Hamish couldn't believe what he was hearing and stopped her before he heard too many details. He then made a few phone calls and summoned Eric. After a rather one-sided and heated argument, Eric was dismissed from his position at Strathbole Castle, but not before agreeing to move to a new position with a family in Germany the following day, never to return to Scotland. Lord Strathbole made it very clear that if he ever did, the consequences would be dire.

Young Eric's upbringing meant he felt he had betrayed his employer and indeed his profession, so he agreed to whatever punishment was meted out. It could be worse; at least he was still going to have a job. If a butler couldn't be trusted around the ladies of the house he was finished, and Eric didn't know any other trade. His only regret was leaving Lady Fiona behind to the mercy of his Lordship. Eric had grown more than fond of her and knew that if she had been unhappy before, she was going to be truly miserable now. As he packed his belongings for a hasty transfer to Europe he could find no way within his sense of duty and honour to help protect her. With a heavy heart and a feeling of failure he headed off the next day, vowing to make a fresh start, learn German and concentrate all his efforts, one way or another, on the staff of his new position.

For her part, Lady Fiona was distraught. Eric had been the one ray of light in her marriage to Hamish and now he was gone for good. Her husband used her infidelity as an excuse to greatly increase his own and their lives became almost entirely separate. Worst still, Lady Fiona discovered soon after Eric's departure that she was pregnant and that the child was almost certainly not Hamish's; almost certainly, but not quite. On the evening of Eric's dismissal Hamish and Fiona had made love, although that expression hardly described the activity with any degree of accuracy. It did however, provide a chance that Fiona might be carrying her husband's child. When Simon Peter was born, the family and staff celebrated as if nothing were wrong, and no more was ever said about the matter.

Fiona doted on the boy and he gave her a new lease of life for a while. Lord Strathbole, however, had not finished punishing her for her betrayal. He slowly but surely replaced all the staff at the Castle and would even have removed her own family staff if Lady Fiona's mother had not stepped in and insisted they remained. As soon as Simon was old enough Hamish sent him off to boarding school, leaving his mother devastated.

With all but a few of her previous staff around and with Simon Peter away and hating boarding school, Fiona turned to drink for solace. At first it was simply extra refills at dinner in the evenings but this was soon augmented with drinks before the meal and after various other increments became drinks before breakfast in order to face the day. She withdrew from her social and charitable commitments, often after embarrassing incidents, and eventually lived almost exclusively within the Castle and its grounds. Friends and family would sympathise with Hamish and compliment him on his patience with Fiona and her little problem.

Chapter Sixteen: The German Count

Technically, Eric Ramsay's new German employer could never legally use the term Count in his home country. The Weimar Republic had banned such usage in 1919. Despite this, and although he never used the term on official correspondence, he was always known as the Count both at home and abroad. Kurt Hessen von Oxburg also looked the part and lived a life that many other European aristocrats could only dream of. His family owned a number of magnificent Schloss throughout Germany and, through a well-planned 19th Century marriage, two castles in Northern Italy. They had invested in industry when many of their counterparts elsewhere invested in large areas of land. The land may have looked lovely compared to the factories of the von Oxburgs but it never produced the same scale of income. The family had huge investments in cars, shipping and chemicals, but derived far more from the outright ownership of the world's second largest producer of coloured pencils, the world's third largest manufacturer of coat hangers and a half share in the fourth largest supplier of spark plugs in Europe. As the value of land fluctuated so did the income derived from it; industry, however, pumped out regular and growing profits for the owners, before, during and after the Second World War.

Kurt had been born shortly after the war ended and had grown up in a castle greatly adapted to his father's needs after he had been badly injured in the second battle of El Alamein. His father lived on the ground floor and as young Kurt grew up he quickly realised his father's main desire was peace and quiet within the living areas. Kurt was most popular with his father if he appeared briefly at breakfast to wish his father good morning then disappeared out of doors until it was time to briefly wish his father good night. Any noise from playing indoors resulted in reprimands and loss of privileges. Kurt never knew whether his father loved him or not, as they never spent enough time together for him to find out. He did, however, develop a love of the great outdoors from his early banishment to the grounds of the family home. Hunting, shooting and fishing became preoccupations as soon as he was able to participate in each, and a series of uncles and cousins instructed him as he grew up.

When his father eventually died of his wartime injuries, some twenty years after the war ended, young Kurt inherited the duties of running the family estate and business interests and quickly adapted their stewardship so that he could hunt, shoot and fish throughout the world with unlimited funds and no troublesome daily duties. On one of his rare trips to Britain he found himself in the company of Hamish Strathbole whilst shooting pheasants in Scotland. The two men discussed many things during the visit, hunting, shooting and fishing included, along with the superiority of the British butler. Whilst never actually close friends, they had kept in touch over the years since first meeting and Lord Strathbole had regarded Kurt's German home as the ideal place to get rid of Eric Ramsay when he discovered Lady Fiona's liaison with the butler.

It was to the von Oxburg's Schloss that Eric had travelled after leaving Strathbole Castle, and there had tried to re-establish himself as the perfect gentleman's gentleman, if only initially as assistant butler. Kurt already had a butler who accompanied him around the world, even on his many hunting trips to Africa, and so Eric was left as de facto butler in the family home in Bavaria for most of the year. Had Kurt been made aware of the real reason for Eric's transfer he might have chosen to take him with him while hunting and left Helmut, the older and steadier family servant, in Germany with the countess and their staff. Had he known everything which happened in his absence above and below stairs he may have had something other than Cape buffalo in the sights of his hunting rifles. Fortunately for all concerned he remained blissfully unaware of all the real dangers in his life as he tracked down big game in the bush and Jungles of Africa.

In due course Kurt and his wife Brunhilda, Hilda for short, had a perfectly balanced family with a son, Otto, being followed two years later by a daughter named Sonia. Kurt travelled the globe far less than before and doted on his children. When at home, he would lavish his attention on them in a way he had never experienced with his own father. He taught them to ride, to shoot, to swim in the river and to ski on the family's annual pilgrimage to Klosters. Helmut re-established himself as the stern ruler of the family seat and Eric was moved to a minor family summer home in Alsace and largely forgotten about by all concerned. The von Oxburgs became an almost deliriously happy family who spent most of their time together whenever possible and were the envy of all who met them. This happy state of affairs may well have lasted forever if, many years later, the Strathboles had not decided to go skiing at Klosters one year instead of their usual trip to Val-d'Isère.

Chapter Seventeen: Two Sons go Skiing

Otto grew into a tall and handsome young man. Even
without his family wealth, he would have been attractive
to the many young women he met whilst riding, shooting
or skiing. In his first year at university he had joined one
of the many duelling clubs and had acquired a scar down
one cheek. His mother was livid, complaining that he had
ruined his boyish good looks. His father laughed it off
and described it as a mark of manhood. The scar added a
hint of mystique and danger to his persona and did his
chances with the opposite sex no harm whatever.

One year, quite by chance, the von Oxburgs and the
Strathboles had booked into the same hotel in Klosters to
take advantage of some early snow. They may well have
passed each other on the slopes or waiting for the chair
lift during the first few days of their holidays, but there
had been no initial recognition of having met previously.
Lady Fiona skied briefly on the first two days and
thereafter retired to her room for most of the visit; her
activities being restricted thereafter, to downhill après
skiing with the help of the mini-bar in their suite. The
countess spent her day with Sonia who was still in her
mid-teens and had become addicted to snowboarding,
much to her father's initial distaste. When it became clear

to him that this was in fact a proper Olympic sport now and his daughter was becoming very good at it, he warmed to the idea and employed a professional trainer who worked under the watchful eye of his wife. This left Kurt and Otto free to ski on- and off-piste as they wished.

On the third day of the von Oxburg's holiday Sonia had a bad fall and broke her ankle. After having it set in the local hospital and moping round the hotel for two days it was decided that mother and daughter would return home, where the family doctor and a team of German specialists could supervise a full recovery with enough physiotherapy to avoid permanent damage to Sonia's sporting aspirations. So it was that Otto and Kurt found themselves in Klosters with the prospect of ten days or so unencumbered by the female members of their family. For their part, Hamish and Simon Peter Strathbole might as well have been there alone for all the involvement poor Fiona had in the holiday.

In the middle of their holidays, after a fine day's skiing, both groups returned to the hotel and agreed separately to meet in the bar for a drink before dinner. Hamish showered and changed quickly, despite the stiffness in his knees and hips. He was keen to join the throng in the bar which always included a fair smattering of young female skiers and chalet maids. Dressed both casually and expensively, he made sure he had a large wad of crisp 50 euro notes in his jacket pocket to pay for drinks.

He could easily have added everything to the bill for the suite but he knew from years of experience that bundles of cash were more attractive to some young ladies, especially impoverished chalet maids reliant on tips. After asking his wife if she cared to join him, out of habit, and receiving no answer from the comatose bundle on the bed he headed downstairs for the bar with a spring in his step which belied the aches in his leg muscles.

As he entered the bar he looked round and was surprised to see that Simon had beaten him to it and was already chatting to two lovely young blondes. "That's my boy," he thought to himself as he made his way over and said "hello".

As the young man turned round, Hamish was embarrassed to see that it was not in fact Simon. The height, build and hair were indeed the same but this lad was younger and had a prominent scar on his left cheek. He was also obviously German when he said: "I beg your pardon?"

"I'm terribly sorry, I mistook you for my son," apologised a rather flustered Lord Strathbole. "You look surprisingly alike from a distance," and he turned away to order a drink.

"Not just from a distance," he thought. This youth was the spitting image of Simon Peter. He even had those dark eyebrows which were completely at odds with the mane of golden hair. In almost every respect the two youngsters were identical, apart from a five year or so gap in ages.

Hamish kept sneaking a glimpse of the young man who was starting to feel quite uncomfortable at the attention but seemed confident enough within himself not to move or indeed look away.

After a further twenty minutes Simon joined his father and ordered a beer. The young German had continued to look over at Lord Strathbole, not entirely unconvinced that the man was trying to pick him up. When he saw Simon arrive though, he realised how the older man had been mistaken. Apart from a slightly heavier build and the lack of a scar, the son was his double. He even had the mismatched eyebrows which Otto hated so much.

Simon looked around the crowded bar while he waited for his drink to see what the talent was like that evening. When his eyes fell on Otto he did a double take.

"There's a bloke over there looks just like me, Hamish," he said.

"I know, son; I even mistook him for you. Bit embarrassing really. He took it in good part though, despite being German."

"If he wasn't a bit younger you would think we were separated at birth," continued a clearly fascinated Simon.

"I was at your birth and I can assure you that you were mercifully on your own. He is the spitting image though."

Ten minutes after Simon had arrived, Kurt joined his son in the bar and ordered a drink for Otto and his new lady-friends. When Hamish saw Kurt he recognised him straight away and the penny dropped. A particularly bad penny which he had hoped he had seen the last of some twenty years previously.

Kurt looked round the bar and saw Hamish. He knew that the face was familiar but could not immediately place it. The two men nodded to each other politely and Kurt was about to return to the conversation of his group when he saw Simon. He too did a double take, as he thought for a split second that he was looking at his own son, before realising that was impossible. Otto was standing right beside him but he even checked this to make doubly sure.

Intrigued, he made his way over to Lord Strathbole and fortunately recognised him on the way.

"Hamish, isn't it?" he asked stretching out a hand as he did so.

"Yes, Kurt. This is my son Simon Peter."

Simon politely shook hands.

"That is my son Otto over there," said Kurt signalling for his son to join them. "Although for a second I thought that my son had been standing with you."

"I'm rather afraid I made the same mistake with young Otto earlier."

Otto joined the group, having promised to meet up with the girls later. He shook hands politely with both Hamish and with Simon Peter but found it difficult to stop staring at the younger of the two men.

"Hamish and I met whilst fishing and shooting in Scotland," Kurt explained. "We haven't actually seen each other for many years. I thought we could dine together as we have all been abandoned by our ladies."

"Of course," agreed Otto. "I would be fascinated to hear all about your past shooting and fishing trips. I'm sure Simon would also be interested in any shared history our families may have."

There followed a rather strange meal which saw all four men discuss skiing, fishing, shooting riding - in fact, anything at all except the elephant in the room. Nobody mentioned the fact that Simon Peter and Otto were not only the spitting image of each other but were almost certainly related. The younger men were going over in their minds which of the two older men at the table was actually their father and which was the cuckold. Hamish was quietly seething at the cheek of his former butler Eric and the weakness of his wife. Kurt for his part was confused. He knew for a fact that he was not Simon Peter's father and was also sure that he and his wife had not been anywhere near Scotland around the time that Otto had been conceived. He had always trusted his wife implicitly and could think of no reason for her to have a liaison with Lord Strathbole; indeed she had found him rather vulgar when she had met him in Scotland all those years before.

When the meal was over, the young men headed back to the bar, ostensibly to meet up with the young ladies from earlier in the evening, leaving the older men together with glasses of brandy.

After a pause Hamish began, "You are probably curious about our sons."

"Something of an understatement, Hamish. They are peas from the proverbial same pod, are they not." Kurt could not hide an edge of anger in his voice.

"I'm afraid I was not entirely honest with you in the past."

"Go on," said Kurt as his anger grew.

"When I sent Ramsay to Germany, it was not a favour to provide you with a British butler."

"Who?" asked Kurt, confused at the mention of the name.

"My butler, Eric Ramsay."

"What's he got to do with this?" asked Kurt.

"Don't you see?"

Kurt had lost the thread of the conversation now. "I sent Eric to our holiday home years ago when Hilda and I started a family. Helmut was a far better butler and you can't have two in the same house. It's like having two women in the same kitchen; it just wouldn't work. But I don't see what he has to do with anything."

"Don't you remember what he looks like? The eyebrows?"

"To be honest, Hamish, I left him at home most of the time when I went hunting and didn't pay him much attention. I left him to look after the staff and Hilda while I was away."

"So did I, and he did a lot more than look after our wives while we were gone. That's why I sacked him. I heard a rumour that he was sleeping with my wife. Isn't it obvious? He must have slept with yours too."

A couple at the next table raised their eyebrows as Hamish finished his sentence rather louder than he had planned.

Kurt pulled himself upright in his chair and stared at Hamish.

"If you are suggesting that my wife had an affair with a servant I will have to ask you to step outside! How dare you?" he bellowed, as the couple next to them deliberately looked away.

"I know exactly how you feel, old boy. I could have killed him when I discovered what was going on between him and Fiona. But he must have done the same in Germany. Look at our sons. The eyebrows, for fuck sake."

The neighbouring couple summoned a waiter and asked to move tables at this point.

Kurt wracked his brains. To be honest, he had been surprised when Eric was offered as a member of staff but had been too polite to refuse the transfer, as Hamish had insisted at the time that it was to confirm the superiority of British butlers once and for all. He hadn't paid much attention to Eric when he arrived and was away for most of his early years of service. Then Helmut had almost insisted on Eric's removal from the castle when Otto was due. The only brief sight he had had of Eric recently had been of a prematurely grey, rather overweight figure who looked as if he drank too much. As he thought though, he did manage to conjure up a picture of the young butler on his arrival from Scotland and now remembered the distinctive dark eyebrows; the same eyebrows sported now by both Otto and Simon Peter.

"Scheisse!" was all he could manage as he slumped back in his chair.

"Exactly, old boy; Scheisse. Either way, while the boys may have their suspicions, we tell them nothing about who their real father is until we decide what to do about it. Agreed?"

"Agreed."

Chapter Eighteen: Peas in a Pod

Otto and Simon made their way to the bar, ignoring the girls Otto had been speaking to before dinner, much to their disappointment. The girls had rather liked the idea of dating brothers.

After they both had a drink in their hands, Simon broke the shocked silence.

"It rather looks like one of our fathers is in fact both of our fathers, as it were. A lot more than shooting and fishing must have gone on back then."

"I have to agree with you, although I am not sure which option I wish to be the case. That my father cheated on my mother or that my mother cheated on him. I fear that my father, Kurt, is to blame. He is nearer our height and neither of us really looks like Hamish."

"I would agree if my father hadn't been shagging for Scotland since puberty. Your father seems so proper and... well ...German."

"Germans are perfectly capable of being lovers too, you know, although I am not sure that applies to my father. The real question is: what do we do now? Whichever of our mothers has been wronged, she must never know."

"I'm not sure mine would understand any of it these days. She has a bit of a problem with the old sauce."

Otto looked confused. "Sauce for the goose?"

"No; the old vino collapso," corrected Simon, indicating with his own glass.

"Oh, I'm sorry. Though having met your father, perhaps our father, I can understand."

Simon was about to take offence when he realised that actually, Otto was spot on.

"We have two options as far as I can see. We could confront our fathers outright and ask them. They must know and may be arguing about it even as we speak, or we can arrange for DNA tests to be carried out. It's fairly routine, nowadays, as long as you have clean samples. It shouldn't be too difficult to organise. We get samples of our own examined then swipe some hair from our fathers while they still have some. The results should confirm things once and for all. What do you say?"

Otto was deep in thought but nodded in agreement.

"I want to find out exactly what happened and, my newly found Scottish brother, who our father really is. In the meantime act as if nothing is amiss. Now I would like to introduce you to Emily and Jennifer over there, who are spending the season in Klosters, cleaning chalets."

Chapter Nineteen: Splitting Hairs

The rest of the holiday went well, with all four men dining together each evening. The older two were both relieved and suspicious that their sons never mentioned the uncanny resemblance to each other. For their part the fathers kept the topics light and never mentioned the time they had spent together as young, newly married men.

On the last evening of the Strathboles' holiday, Otto and Simon met in the bar before dinner, foregoing the busy bar itself for a quiet alcove. Otto produced four envelopes marked A, B, C and D. A and B were already sealed and he handed C and D to Simon who took a clump of grey hair from his right pocket and sealed it in envelop C. He then took a clump of golden hair from his left pocket, sealed it in envelop D before handing both back to Otto. The German carefully placed the four envelopes into the inside pocket of his jacket.

"I'll take them to a research laboratory I know in Germany. They carry out DNA testing as a sideline, for the police and to settle paternity cases mainly, and I will phone you as soon as I get the results. Then we will find out if we are in fact brothers and indeed who our father is."

They toasted the plan and made their way back to the bar where Kurt and Hamish were talking in quiet tones, almost like conspirators.

The rest of the evening passed in the usual good humour with tall tales of skiing and other exploits over dinner before the younger men made excuses to head for the bar. When they were safely out of earshot, the two older men turned to each other with a business-like air.

"What should we do about this Ramsay character?" began Kurt.

"Well we can't risk anybody finding out about this, least of all him," replied Hamish. "Think of the scandal, not to mention the legal implications for our sons if it becomes public that they are our butler's sons. If he finds out it leaves us both open to blackmail. Didn't it ever dawn on you when you saw them both?"

"Ramsay was sent away to our summer house in Alsace years ago and we haven't been there since as a family. My cousins have used it sometimes but I only visited again very recently while on business and Ramsay looks nothing like he once did. He is grey and heavy now and drinks too much."

"Well we need a permanent solution to this problem to ensure that nobody ever finds out. Fortunately the boys seem completely disinterested. "

"What do you mean, 'a permanent solution'?"

"I mean that Ramsay has to disappear for good, one way or another, and life for our families can go on uninterrupted, old boy. This is not the time for faint hearts. What would your father or grandfather have done if they had found out one of the staff had slept with their wives?"

Kurt pictured his grandmother, and thought it highly unlikely, but had to admit, "They would have shot the bugger and thought nothing more about it."

"Exactly, old boy."

Kurt looked at Hamish and realised that they had begun to formulate a plan.

"We must never discuss this again, but I'm attending 'The Butlers Ball' shortly in Edinburgh. Make sure Ramsay attends and I'll see to the rest once I see his name on the guest list. Agreed?"

Kurt nodded, thinking about his Hilda and the grey old man in the castle in Alsace

"Agreed."

Chapter Twenty: The Results

Otto had decided to hear the results of the DNA testing personally, not wanting to risk word of them leaking out at the Schloss. He made an appointment on the morning the results would be available and arrived early, now desperate for clarification as to who his real father was: Kurt or Hamish. Secretly he hoped it was Kurt, as he had not been impressed by Lord Strathbole. His head, though, suggested Kurt was unlikely to have strayed while visiting Scotland so soon after marriage to his mother, which made Hamish the likely villain of the piece, tragically, along with his beloved mother, Hilda.

He was shown into a large office in the administrative block of the factory and found a middle aged man in a white lab coat waiting for him.

"I'm Doctor Brunner," said the scientist. "It is a pleasure to meet you Herr von Oxburg."

"Otto," Otto insisted.

The doctor looked his client up and down quickly and decided it was a fairly typical paternity issue, unusual only in so far as there were four people involved. No doubt either this young man had doubts of his child's origins or had been sowing his wild oats, and was now being brought to account for his past pleasures. No matter, the results were here now and all would be revealed.

Dr Brunner had not had time to read the results before the meeting but was sure they would play out in one of the ways he had predicted. He opened a file which sat on his desk and read through the details with a slight raising of his eyebrows as he did so.

"Otto, you asked us to test four samples to ascertain any genetic like between the individuals involved with particular regard to any sibling relationship or paternity, is that correct?"

"It is."

"The testing has been carried out and we have very clear results to the questions you wish answered, although I am slightly confused. In detail then: sample A and sample D have a very close match and are almost certainly siblings, brothers to be exact. There is however, no other genetic connection between the samples."

"I don't understand," said Otto. "There must be a connection."

"No, I am quite sure there is not. Sample A and D are very closely related as I say but there is no similarity between samples B and C."

"I know that," interrupted Otto, "But B or C must be related to both A and D."

Dr Brunner doubted his own interpretation of the results in front of him for a second and re-read them slowly.

"No, there is no doubt in the matter. B is not related to A, C or D and C is not related to A, B or D. The results are quite conclusive. Is this not what you were expecting?"

"Not at all," said a rather stunned Otto, trying to make sense of the news. "B is a good guy and was unlikely to be related to A and D but C is a real bastard who had paternity of A and D written all over his face. Now I need to track down sample E."

"We were not given a fifth sample denoted E," said Dr Brunner, now completely confused.

"Not yet you haven't, but you will."

Dr Brunner handed a copy of the results to Otto who read them again to make sure he had fully grasped the implications. He had. He and Simon were definitely brothers but neither Hamish nor Kurt was their father. He thanked the doctor vaguely and left the office still in a state of confusion.

It took him a further thirty minutes before he phoned Simon on his mobile as agreed.

"Did you get the results then," Simon asked straight away. "Are we Scottish or German?"

"We may be neither, I am afraid, although we are definitely brothers, sons of the same father. Unfortunately though, neither of our fathers is our father so to speak."

"What, are you sure? There must be a mistake with the results."

"There is no mistake. As long as you got a sample of Hamish's hair it means that we are neither von Oxburgs nor Strathboles. A fact that we must ensure remains our little secret. The laboratory has no names attached to the samples."

"It was definitely my dad's hair, not of course that he is my dad it appears, but it came from Hamish's hair brush."

"So, what do we do now?"

"We have to keep this completely to ourselves, as you say. The only way forward is to find out who our mothers slept with all those years ago, although my mother may have difficulty remembering."

"I have no intention of asking my mother. Hilda is one of the best shots in Bavaria and has a short fuse at the best of times. We have to be a bit more subtle about this.

There must be people we can ask who were around at the time and might have at least heard whispers?"

"There are very few servants at the castle from that time except my mother's two closest maids who wouldn't give anything away even if you tortured them. They are too loyal. The only other possibility is Nanny MacPhee, her real name's Nanny MacIntosh, but whether she was aware of any shenanigans or not is doubtful. I'll give it a try though. What about your side of things?"

"As far as I am aware," said Otto, "Your folks never stayed at the Schloss. Their only meetings were in Scotland for the fishing and shooting. It must have happened there, or there must be a mutual friend who stayed at both and charmed the pants off our mothers, quite literally. I'll see what I can find out. I suggest we hold a conference call this time tomorrow."

"Agreed," said Simon and the two men hung up, lost thereafter in their own thoughts.

Chapter Twenty One: Nanny MacPhee gets a visitor

Simon drove himself from Edinburgh to Strathbole Castle, deep in thought all the way. The revelations of the morning had left him reeling. He had been so sure that his father Hamish was indeed his father and therefore Otto's father too that he had never considered any other possibility. He had even ruled out Kurt being the father of both sons on the grounds of his formal and rather boring outlook on life. Now he had to come to terms not only with the fact that he was not Hamish's son, but also that his mother had been unfaithful to his father with his real father - whoever he might be. It was all a jolt to the calm and sheltered life he was used to.

He was not overly confident of gaining any information from his former nanny. His memories of her all centred round the laying down of a fairly strict code of conduct based on such high moral principles that he assumed she would have been blind to anyone who broke those rules in the adult household. On the other hand, though, Nanny MacPhee was smart. It didn't matter how hard Simon had tried to hide his misdemeanours as a child, she had always seen through his attempts at covering them up. She had been a central figure in the family for years and had raised Hamish too. She must surely have been able to see through anyone else's attempts at covering up misbehaviour of any kind. If anyone offered a link back to his mother's wayward past it would be her.

After what seemed like ages he arrived at the castle and sneaked in the back door and up to the room where old and now blind Nanny MacPhee spent her days. He immediately felt guilty, like a schoolboy who had missed a birthday or a mealtime and now had to face the music. He knew he hadn't been to see his old Nanny for months, if not years. It had been so long in fact that he had never visited her in the room she now occupied in order to be looked after by the other staff. The last time he had gone to see her she had still been in the two rooms beside the old nursery. They had met then in the living room, where she had visitors, which adjoined an ensuite bedroom where she slept and where her personal mementos were on display. Since then her legs had failed her in addition to her eyesight and Lady Strathbole's maids had set up her belongings in an ensuite bedroom above the main kitchen, with plenty of staff around her at all times. She had been reluctant at first to leave the rooms she had called home for so long but was realistic enough to know she could no longer take care of herself.

"It will be one last adventure," she had said as Lady Fiona herself wheeled her in to the new room.

In the end she loved the hustle and bustle around her and wished the move had happened years before. Her old rooms were so quiet without children in the neighbouring nursery or indeed without anybody around for long periods of time. Now she was in danger of drowning from too many cups of tea and had put on weight from the biscuits which always accompanied them.

Simon Peter knocked gently on the door, a guilty knock which his old nanny immediately recognised.

"Simon Peter, is that you?"

"Yes Nanny, it's me. Sorry I haven't visited for a while."

"Nonsense, you have so much living to do at your age you have no place visiting an old fossil like me too often, though I'm delighted you are here now and can tell me all your news."

"I've asked Annie to bring up tea and scones. How do you like your new room?" Simon asked, feeling at ease with his nanny as he always did. She had always managed to put him at his ease.

"I love to hear all the hustle and bustle around me without having to help," Nanny MacPhee laughed. "I'm glad you popped in. You must tell me everything going on in your life at the moment. Except all the girls, I trust you to leave out the sordid details of your love life."

Simon blushed as if he were still only ten. He realised he had missed her, and felt even more guilty that his only reason for this visit was to try and pick her brains about his mother's past and to try to discover who had fathered both himself and Otto.

"I should visit more often, I'm sorry."

"If you came more often we would have nothing to talk about. Anyway, how is the big bad world?"

"As big and bad as ever really. We all went skiing recently in Klosters. The snow was very good for so early in the season. Mother didn't ski much of course, but Father and I were out all day every day."

"Your poor mother. She didn't make a scene or anything, did she?"

"No, not this time. She spent most of her time in the hotel room really, so it was alright." Then after a pause Simon asked, "Did she always drink as much, Nanny?"

"Not at first; not straight after the wedding. Your father is a difficult man to live with at times, as you know, but she was happy here at the castle at first. I remember her remodelling the gardens and arranging for the main rooms to be decorated. Yes, she hardly drank at all when she was happy "

"What made her so unhappy? Was it all my father's doing?"

Simon found he could be completely honest with his old nanny, and in return she would always be honest with him when she could.

"He was perhaps the main reason. He was away a lot and there were rumours of his behaviour in London and Edinburgh which upset your mother terribly, but she was still happy here. It was almost as if it were her family home rather than your father's. The staff here took to her so well. I think she must have suffered depression when she was expecting you. I seem to remember her going into moods about that time, although she was thrilled when you were born. Andrew had just taken over as butler after that unfortunate business with Eric and the trainee cook, and I remember him calling in Doctor MacDonald on a regular basis."

"I thought Andrew had always been here."

"He has been here since before you were born, but only just."

"So mother started drinking after I was born?"

"Not immediately. It started after your father sent you off to boarding school. Your mother begged him not to, and I even joined in, but his mind was set on making your mother unhappy and he went ahead. Your mother and I realised you were very unhappy there and it broke her heart. You were far too young to be away all the time. I think missing you was the start of it really."

Annie arrived with the tea and Simon looked around the room while she served it. The room was big enough for someone who could hardly move but it appeared cluttered by the large number of ornaments and photographs, now all useless to their owner. He recognised the picture of the family with Churchill, which she was so proud of, along with pictures of staff, and of the family with the staff over the years. He even noticed one with himself and the staff outside the walled garden. Remembrances of happy times now lost to his poor nanny. He turned back to the tea tray and buttered a scone for Nanny MacPhee.

"Weren't Lucy and Janette able to cheer mother up?" he asked referring to the two maids who had transferred to the castle when his mother married Hamish.

"Of course they tried their best, but she was inconsolable. She missed you so much and lost all interest in the garden and the house. Fortunately Andrew took over and paid far more attention to such things than that rascal Eric had."

"There must have been lots of visitors to entertain; that must have been a diversion for her."

"The castle used to be such a centre for entertaining, especially in your grandfather's day. I've told you about Churchill visiting, for example."

"He didn't visit shortly before I was born, did he, before making a grand tour of Bavaria ?"

"No, of course not. He was here in the 50s. That's your father as a baby in the picture there. Churchill died long before you were born. Why ever did you ask?"

"Oh, just a long shot really. What about German visitors?"

"There were very few, what with the war and all that. The only ones I remember were a rather stuffy couple from Bavaria who had just got married and came here to fish and shoot. Your father was doing some business with the Count; something to do with coloured pencils for Scottish schools. He was very formal and she was a beauty, if I remember. She was also a very good shot. Your father was worried she might clear the grounds of pheasants that year."

"Was that just before I was born, then?"

Nanny MacPhee thought for a while before answering.

"It would have been three years or so before you came along." The old lady seemed to check her memory again as she often did these days to confirm the accuracy of her recollection. "Yes, definitely around three years before you arrived."

"Did my folks ever visit the von Oxburgs in Germany?"

"That was their name, Simon, how clever you are! No, I don't think so. Once Hamish got his pencils for the school contract he dropped them, although they must have kept in touch to an extent."

"How do you know that, Nanny?"

"Well, your father must have. After all, he packed Eric off to work for them when he was caught with Lizzy the young cook. I'm sure your father wouldn't have been quite so cross if they hadn't been found 'at it' in the larder. Cook was raging too, food hygiene and all that."

"So Eric was sent off to work for Kurt von Oxburg?"

"Yes, as assistant butler I believe; served the scoundrel right."

"When would that have been?"

"That would have been around the time you were born. Just before, in fact, as Andrew dealt with all the arrangements for your mother's confinement."

"You don't happen to have a picture of Eric by any chance?"

"He's in one of the ones over there: the large picture of the senior staff at the entrance to the walled garden. That would have been a year or two before you were born."

Simon looked over at the collection of photographs on the old lady's dressing table. His eyes fell on the one with himself and the staff. Then he did a double take. It wasn't a picture of himself and the staff, it couldn't be. Nanny MacPhee was standing upright and looked thirty or so years younger than she did now. Simon stared at the young butler beside her, at his broad shoulders, his golden mane of hair and at his strangely dark eyebrows and knew he was staring at his father.

"Did Mother like Eric Ramsay ?" he asked, in as calm a voice as he could muster.

His old nanny paused.

"She was fond of him, yes. They even played tennis together. He was an accomplished player, as was your mother."

"Bingo!" said Simon.

"No dear, tennis; not the same thing at all. I wouldn't say this to anybody else, but there were scurrilous rumours about them which I am sure were entirely unfounded. Your mother would never have had anything to do with the staff, and certainly not the likes of Eric Ramsay."

"I wouldn't be so sure," Simon thought to himself.

He stood up and slowly and gently kissed his nanny on her forehead.

"Thank you Nanny MacPhee, I could always rely on you to help me when I needed it."

"You're welcome, Simon. Come and see me again when you can."

Simon walked slowly down the stairs, through the kitchen and outside towards the walled garden. The revelation that he was the illegitimate son of a disgraced butler was something of a shock. He wondered how Otto would take the news; after all he was only the son of an assistant butler. He was certain that even a German would have preferred Churchill.

Chapter Twenty Two: Otto hears the bad news

Simon made his way into the walled garden and over to the hexagonal summer house that stood in the warmest corner. The wooden building was unlocked as usual, when the public weren't touring the grounds, and he went inside. Sitting on the swing seat that he had always loved as a child during his brief respites at home away from the bullying and abuse of boarding school, he took out his mobile phone and phoned Otto.

"Otto? Are you sitting down?"

"Why, what have you got for me?"

"I know who our father is." Simon paused.

"How did you find that out? I take it your Nanny spilled the tin of beans. Who is it, don't keep me in suspense!"

"It appears that our butler was sacked not long before I was born for messing about with a young cook."

"What's that got to do with us?" asked Otto impatiently.

"Stop interrupting! For years I wanted a brother, and now I find they are a pain in the neck. The butler was a bit of a ladies' man and there were rumours of an affair with my mother at the time."

115

Again Simon paused.

"Get on with it. You are right that brothers can be a pain."

"Well my father sent him away as far as he could when he found out, which unfortunately was only as far as Bavaria. Your butler, Eric Ramsay, is our father."

Otto laughed, "Our butler is called Helmut and is the last person on earth either of our mother's would have anything to do with. You have been misinformed."

"Not your butler then. Your assistant butler."

"We don't have one."

"You must have or at least did have years ago. Maybe your father sacked him too or shot him or something but he is the one. He has our eyebrows; I've just looked at a photo of him almost thirty years ago when he worked here and it could have been either of us today."

There was a pause at the other end of the line as Otto thought things through.

"The name means nothing to me, and there is no one on our staff with our eyebrows, believe me, or I would have noticed before now. Let me ask around and I'll let you know if this Ramsay person made it to Germany. I'll speak to you soon."

Simon ended the call and put his phone down. His mind was a swirling mess of confusion and contradictions. He had hated his childhood at boarding school and always blamed his parents for sending him away. As he grew older he had assumed his father had made the decision to spare him the embarrassment of his mother's drunken scenes. A new version of events was taking form within his head now, though: One where his father had always known or suspected what had happened and was determined to punish all concerned. But why had his mother had anything to do with the butler? She had had everything she could have possibly wanted. Or had she? There was only one way of finding out. He had to ask his mother and catch her early enough in the day for her to make sense.

Six hundred miles away, Otto was also deep in thought. He had been prepared for Hamish to have been his father or for Kurt to be Simon Peter's father. That would not have been so unusual within aristocratic circles. If it proved true that a butler had fathered them both then it was quite a different matter. Apart from the sheer embarrassment of it there were all sorts of legal questions raised for both the men regarding their inheritances. Of course it may still be a red herring. He had never heard of Eric Ramsay and could not remember anyone in the household with the same ill matching hair and eyebrow combination he shared with his new-found Scottish brother.

He would ask around very carefully to see if Ramsay had ever served at the Schloss, but whatever he did he would have to make sure his mother never discovered his line of questioning. She was as sharp as a razor from the moment she got up until the moment she went to bed and nothing happened in her household without her knowing about it, generally from the ever loyal Helmut.

Chapter Twenty Three: Lady Fiona's Admission

The following day Simon rose early and had a quick breakfast before insisting on carrying his mother's breakfast tray up to her room. Lady Fiona was both surprised and pleased to see her son first thing in the morning but also a little confused; there again, being a little confused was her natural state at that time of the day.

He poured her a large cup of coffee and buttered a piece of croissant before pouring himself a cup of coffee and joining her by sitting on the side of the bed.

"Is it Mother's Day?" asked Lady Fiona in all honesty.

"Not today," replied Simon. "I thought I would spoil you for once while I am here."

Simon leaned over and kissed his mother on the top of her head. If she had been more aware of life around her she might have become suspicious at that point, but her addled brain had long since lost its ability to recognise subterfuge.

"That's nice," she said, genuinely thinking it was a more pleasant start to the day than she had had for some time.

"You always seem unhappy these days, I wanted to try and cheer you up," said Simon.

"Oh things aren't so bad really," countered his mother. "Not once the gin kicks in."

At that she laughed showing a hint of her old sense of humour.

"Were you always so unhappy, Mother?"

She looked at him with a questioning but entirely unsuspicious look, as if touched by the question and wondering if he really wished an honest answer or was only making polite conversation. She must have decided that he genuinely wanted to know and opened up just a little bit, pleased to have her only child by her side.

"I was happy years ago. Happy at first when I married your father, I suppose. But he was never here. I was happy once with the gardens here and the bustle of castle life; it was so like my own home for a while. The staff here were so kind. They helped keep me sane, I suppose, while your father was away doing who knows what... with who knows who."

"Andrew seems a solid bloke. He must have been a comfort when you were here on your own as a young bride."

Lady Fiona looked at him, wondering why his statement made no sense to her. It was all such a long time ago and everyone had changed since then. But there was more to it than just that. What was it? There was something in Simon's words which had stopped her train of thought, but she couldn't quite place it. She had been happy then, she knew it, but her damaged brain couldn't quite grasp the details. Andrew was a solid bloke but he wasn't the kind to make her feel comfortable. He was very much Hamish's man. He lacked the compassion needed to rally the staff around her when she was lonely. She looked at Simon sitting on the side of her bed; the golden mop of hair flopping down one side of his face. His curiously incongruous black eyebrows and those broad shoulders, offering comfort and a defence against the world. A tear formed in her eye and Simon leaned forward to hug her.

"Hold me again, Eric," she whispered. "Let me feel safe again just for a minute or two."

Simon held her and felt tears form in his eyes too. His mother must have been so unhappy and lonely. It didn't justify her actions perhaps, but he could understand them better now: a lonely and wronged bride in a castle without her prince charming. It wasn't entirely surprising that she had sought comfort in the arms of a knave.

<u>Chapter Twenty Four: Otto asks around</u>

"Good morning, Helmut," said Otto. "How are you today?"

"Very well, thank you, sir. I trust you are well. Was your skiing holiday a success?"

"Yes, thank you, very good snow for this stage of the season. There were also some very interesting people there too. That always adds to the experience; Mainly Brits but a few Italians too. One of the British families had an assistant butler, Helmut. Why would anyone have an assistant butler?"

"I can only assume their actual butler is not up to the job," said Helmut in his most snobbish manner.

"We've never had an assistant butler, have we?" continued Otto.

"No sir, of course not. At least, we have never needed one."

"Of course not, Helmut; you would never need help running things here."

"No, sir."

After a pause and a mouthful of coffee Otto reiterated, "So we have never had an assistant butler then?"

Helmut had been used to Otto and his sister asking questions of him almost from the moment they could talk and he had always answered them honestly, if briefly, on the basis that he believed children should be told the truth and therefore only have to learn things once. That old habit died hard and he felt on this occasion that although his young master was essentially now a man, he should answer as honestly as he possibly could.

"We did briefly take on a British servant as an assistant butler while your father was travelling and I was away accompanying him. He was transferred to the Summer Villa years ago when your father gave up big game hunting. The summer villa was about as much as he could manage. I believe he is still there in a more minor role"

"Oh, I didn't know that. What was his name?"

Helmut thought for a moment or two. "Eric, I believe. Eric Ramsay."

Otto hid all emotion from his face.

"Strange people the British, needing two butlers," He said. "Anyway, I think I will go for a long ride today. Would you be kind enough to ask my groom to prepare one of the hunters for me; Ajax, probably, he looks like he needs the exercise."

Helmut nodded and headed off to phone the stables, thinking no more of the conversation and putting Eric Ramsay back where he felt he belonged; at the very back of his mind.

Chapter Twenty Five: The Sons compare notes

Once Otto was a mile or two away from the Schloss and well out of the sight or hearing of any of the staff he telephoned Simon Strathbole on his mobile.

"You were right," he said when Simon answered. "Your father sent Eric Ramsay to us after he had an affair with your mother and he must have done the same here with my mother while my father was shooting anything that moved in East Africa. Helmut took over the reins here when mother was expecting me and Eric was packed off to a summer house we own in Alsace. We never went there afterwards and it became my distant cousins' holiday retreat in effect. Ramsay's still there as far as I can make out but no one here seems to have made the connection, and they mustn't."

"I managed to get a few minutes of sense out of my mother this morning. She certainly remembers young Eric fondly. My father left her alone here too, much of the time. Now what do we do?"

"I don't know. Part of me is curious to meet him. What about you?"

"Yes, in a way. He must have provided some comfort to my mother one way or another. Of course another part of me wants to shoot the rogue and forget everything we have found out. Best if we both sleep on it and chat again in a couple of days. Agreed?"

"Agreed."

The next time the unlikely brother spoke on the phone they had both had time to digest the realisation that they were not the fathers' sons they thought they were and that their mothers had both had more interesting lives than they once thought. A blur of conflicting thoughts and emotions swirled round their heads and never fully resolved themselves. As a result, when next they spoke, both were sure that they had to meet Eric Ramsay before a clear course of action could be chosen.

"What are your thoughts?" asked Simon after the minimum of small talk.

"I would like to at least meet the man before deciding what we do, if anything," Otto replied.

"Me too," agreed Simon. "I don't want to do anything to rock our current boats, as it were, but part of me wants to meet my real father, even if only once. The big problem is doing that without giving the game away. After all, if he has gone from being our butler to being a glorified caretaker in your summer cottage, he may see a way of feathering his nest if he finds out one or more of the wealthiest heirs in Europe are his own flesh and blood."

"I agree but I have an idea how we can manage to see him without him realising who we really are," said Otto.

"Really? Go on."

"Well, it strikes me that he has never met either of us and is presumably unaware of our relationship. All I need to do is arrange a pretext to visit our house in Alsace with my Scottish friend and stay overnight. We would need to disguise ourselves slightly, at least as far as our eyebrows and hair are concerned, but beyond that he needn't be any the wiser. What do you think?"

"You make it sound easy enough but we do rather look alike, even if we dye our eyebrows to match our hair."

"No, we do the opposite: we dye our hair black to match our eyebrows, you wear padding to add a good few kilograms and we both grow beards and moustaches. One of us slouches while he is around and the other wears hidden heels or something and we can both be sufficiently different to fool him for a day."

Simon thought about it for a moment and said, "I'm game if you are. When?"

"No time like the present. I'll arrange to visit for an overnight stay in a few weeks; we could hunt boar or something. You fly to Mulhouse, I'll collect you at the airport, then we head out to the summer house to meet him. I'll take some paperwork that we can use as an excuse to have a more lengthy discussion with him, and afterwards we can see what we think. Agreed?"

"Agreed. I'll work on a disguise and walking with a stoop; you buy some high heels. In the meantime I'll stop shaving and see what the facial growth looks like."

A day was set for the young men to visit Alsace and 'drop in' on their father. Simon Strathbole made an excuse to his father, who didn't care, for being away for a few days and packed hand luggage for the journey, the contents of which consisted mainly of a disguise to hide his similarity to both a young Eric Ramsay and to Otto von Oxburg. He had a friend drive him to the airport from his flat in Edinburgh and, after a difficult moment explaining the contents of his suitcase to a member of airport security during a random search, settled back in the cramped seat of the budget airline plane for the mercifully short flight to Mulhouse. His mind was still very much a maelstrom of conflicting emotions but he was determined now to meet his real father at least this once.

He discovered the in-flight magazine and after two minutes declared it unreadable to the two young students sitting beside him. They remained unmoved by his announcement, deaf as they were due to the headphones in their ears. Knowing that he was being collected and driven to the summer house by Otto, Simon made the most of the in-flight drinks service, having got over the initial surprise that it was not, in fact, free.

After managing three gins and tonic, he dozed off briefly before a stewardess woke him and asked him to put his seat belt back on, ready for the plane's approach and landing. He took a second or two to get his bearings before complying, but belted up as requested.

He made it through passport control without any further embarrassing searches and found Otto waiting for him at the arrivals gate.

They shook hands warmly, now not only brothers, but also conspirators.

"Did you have a good flight?" asked Otto.

"It was budget and lived up to its name. Did you know you have to pay for your drinks on these flights,?" replied Simon.

"I had heard," replied Otto examining his brother's new facial growth with approval. He was also impressed by the effect of his dyed black hair, an effect which he now shared. Rather than disguising the obvious family connection which their unusual eyebrows had given them, the now matching hair made them look even more alike.

"How did you get on with the padding?" Otto asked.

"Don't ask, I had a hell of a job explaining it at Edinburgh airport. The bloke there was unconvinced by my story of a fancy dress party. I've added a pair of horn rim glasses to the ensemble which helps with the transformation. Your beard looks good though, and I see you have gained height. Well done. I'll change somewhere on the way if that's okay? I don't fancy another interview with somebody at the airport. I had to ask for the man's name and supervisor before I got through in Scotland."

"We'll have a bite to eat on the way and you can change there," said Otto. "Then we will find out what our father is really like. I have to admit that I am slightly nervous about the whole thing. You?"

"Yes, unusually. I can't think why, though."

They jumped into Otto's BMW and headed out of the airport. They spoke little on the way, each of them lost in their own thoughts. After an hour or so Otto turned off the autobahn and drove a few miles to a large hotel, which had once been a stately home, Simon judged, by the look of it.

Otto parked his car and the two of them walked into the hotel where the receptionist welcomed Otto as a regular guest, although she realised there was something quite different about him. She looked at Simon for a second, as if surprised to meet Otto's brother for the first time, and seemed even more surprised when the two conversed in English on their way to the dining room. She turned back to her computer screen, though, assuming the young men were engaged in high jinks of some kind.

An immaculately dressed waiter led them to a table while asking Otto a few polite questions, again confirming he was a regular, and, worryingly, not fooled by the disguise.

Once seated and having ordered, they got down to business.

"What's the full cover story for our short visit?" asked Simon.

"You are an old friend from university. We met while you were on an exchange from Oxford. You were going to be in the area and we arranged to meet and go shooting. I am combining the trip with some paperwork which needs to be done to audit the accounts for the household. You will sit in to practice your very rusty German."

"My German is virtually non-existent."

"Don't worry about that; I gather Eric's isn't perfect, so we will no doubt revert to English fairly quickly. You check him out while I go through the stuff I've brought, and then have a natter about Scotland. I have only told him you're from Edinburgh, you can make up the rest from there. We can compare notes this evening after dinner. The only other servant there is his wife who speaks passable English, so be aware. Their two daughters might be about too. They're in their early teens, I think."

"Our half sisters?"

"My God! I never thought of that, but I suppose they are, in a way."

"A very real way, Otto. I wonder what colour their eyebrows are?"

"Don't go there, please!"

The food arrived and the two unlikely brothers ate in silence.

After they had eaten the two of them left the table and Otto engaged the receptionist in conversation while Simon retrieved his case from the car and slipped into the toilet to change. He emerged after twenty minutes or so, a somewhat fuller figure than when he went in, and also sporting unflattering horn-rim glasses. He passed Otto without a word and made his way to the car, unconcerned by the thoughts of any staff who may have seen him before and after. Otto joined him at the car shortly afterwards, unable to stifle a laugh.

"What?" asked Simon.

"I'm sorry, but it does really change you so much! Especially the strange walk you were doing."

"What strange walk? That's the way you walk when you gain twenty kilos in twenty minutes."

They both laughed and Otto gunned the engine as they sped out of the driveway of the hotel and back onto the road for the short journey to the summer house and a meeting with Eric Ramsay.

<u>Chapter Twenty Six: The Summer House</u>

When they arrived there, even Simon was impressed. The term Summer House hardly did it justice. He estimated the three storey building must have around twenty bedrooms or so, not counting staff quarters, with at least six substantial public rooms on the ground floor. It was set in a hundred acres of grounds and was reached via a half mile long driveway which put the autobahns to shame.

"Nice place," said Simon.

"I've never really been before," replied Otto. "I might have to come more often, though. I gather the hunting is first rate."

They drove up to the front door, where a middle aged figure was standing ready to meet them.

"There's Dad, I suppose," said Simon and both men stared at him as they parked the car.

"Good afternoon, gentlemen," said Eric in German. "Did you have a pleasant journey?"

"Yes thank you… Eric," said Otto taking the lead. "This is my friend Mr Smith, from Scotland."

"Pleased to meet you, Mr Smith. I hope you enjoy your stay, short as it."

Eric had switched to English and Simon was aware of a strong Scottish accent still there in his voice.

"I believe you hale from Scotland originally, Eric?"

"I have that honour sir, though I haven't been back for years now. How is God's country?" Eric asked with a hint of emotion in his voice.

"Still the same, I'm afraid. Six months of freezing rain, then we get winter."

The two laughed at that, and Otto joined in without fully understanding the joke.

Eric offered to take the small cases the two younger men had brought in the car but they insisted on carrying them, much to Eric's surprise. Once inside he introduced them to his wife who offered them a bite to eat or some tea, which they politely refused, still full from lunch. Eric then led the way up the stairs to the main bedrooms on the first floor.

"I don't believe you have ever visited the Summer House?" Eric asked Otto in German.

"I believe not," he replied watching Eric intently as he showed them round the first floor.

Once they had seen their rooms, Eric left each of them alone to settle in, having first been asked to meet up with them again in the downstairs study in an hour's time to review the paperwork Otto had brought with him. When he had left, the two visitors met in Otto's room.

"Well, we have now met him. What do you think?" asked Simon.

"Seems a decent enough bloke," replied Otto. "I can't think what our mothers saw in him, though, unless he has piled on the weight since he moved here."

"Of course he has. He has been here for over twenty years, got married, had children and had very little work to do in a largely unused house. The photo I saw of him as a young man at the castle was quite different."

"Anyway, we will find out more about him when I check through these accounts," said Otto. "At least we will find out if he is honest or not."

After unpacking and freshening themselves up, they made their way together to the study. Eric was waiting for them there and had a series of tidy folders spread out on the huge oak desk. As they arrived he stood up and offered them the chairs he had placed beside the desk.

"Thank you, Eric. I hope you don't mind if Mr Smith sits in? He is keen to improve his rather rusty German."

"Of course not, Sir," said Eric, aware he didn't really have a choice in the matter.

For the next hour or so Otto went through the accounts of the Summer House in minute detail while Simon watched Eric answer all the questions with a relaxed confidence that suggested everything was in order, no matter how much Otto decided to dig into the paperwork. Simon was impressed by this and by the thoroughness of Otto's interrogation.

When Otto finally ran out of questions he closed the last of the folders.

"Thank you, Eric. Everything seems to be in fine order. Would it be possible to have coffee now; tea for my friend here perhaps?"

"Coffee is fine," said Simon.

"Very well," said Eric, rising from the table.

"Oh, and Eric? Make that three cups and do join us now that the formal stuff is over."

"Thank you, Sir," said Eric, genuinely pleased at the invitation.

When Eric's wife brought in the tray with cups, coffee pot and homemade gingerbread biscuits she smiled at the young men and was obviously relieved that her husband's running of the household had met with their approval.

"I made these biscuits for your visit. They are to a recipe of my mother's."

"Excellent," said Otto, before translating for Simon.

Simon thanked her kindly in English and tried one of them before she left the study.

"Delicious," he said and watched her beam with pride.

For the following hour or so the three men held a conversation which went from formal discussion of the estate, through polite questions about Eric's daughters, to a more relaxed discussion of the younger men's time at University and their romantic affairs. Eric chipped in a few risqué tales from below stairs and they found themselves laughing and enjoying the conversation far more than they could have expected.

Just as they recovered from a fit of giggles at Simon's story of twin sisters at Oxford there was a knock on the study door. Eric was about to rise to answer it when Otto merely shouted out, "Come in!"

The door opened slowly and a rather nervous little girl of around twelve years old entered the room.

"I am sorry to interrupt," she said in a hesitant voice. "Daddy, you promised we would play a game before dinner and it's getting late."

Simon and Otto stared at the girl. She had golden hair which would have mirrored their own if they hadn't both dyed it black, and it was tied in a tight single pony tail which hung down her back. They were both relieved to note that her eyebrows were also the same golden colour.

"I am sorry gentlemen. This is my daughter Heidi. It was her birthday last week and one of her presents was the game of Cluedo. She has been desperate to play it ever since. I don't know if you are familiar with the game but I did promise to play her today."

"I used to play it with my mother," both young men said almost simultaneously in two languages.

They looked at each other in surprise while Eric looked at them both.

"I haven't played it in years," said Simon. "Could I join in?"

"I was just about to say the same," said Otto.

"I used to play it years ago with... Well in previous circumstances," said Eric. "I'd be delighted if you joined us. It is always better with more players. My wife thinks it's a stupid game and won't play but my other daughter loves it too."

He turned to Heidi and added, "Go and fetch Fiona and we'll join you in the dining room."

"Your other daughter is called Fiona. Not a very German name," said Simon.

"My wife agreed that we would have one British name and then a local name for our children. I always liked the name Fiona," said Eric wistfully, completely unaware of the train of thoughts set in motion within Simon's head.

The three men headed from the office to the dining room where the two sisters were already busy setting up the board game. Fiona was two or three years older than Heidi and was already showing signs of growing into a beauty. She had the same golden hair but wore hers cut short in a bob, which rather suited her slim features.

Heidi took charge of the game and told everyone where to sit. Otto insisted that she started as it was her game, and the five of them embarked on a quest to discover who had killed who, with what and where, with much laughing and joking along the way.

Eric's wife appeared after a while during the second game to ask the girls to leave the visitors in peace and to get ready for dinner, and was surprised when all five of the players protested before agreeing that they would eat together at the table while continuing to play. Completely confused, but seeing that the dreaded visit was going far better than she could have imagined, she agreed and went back to the kitchen to prepare a suitable meal.

The games continued till nine o'clock or so at which point Olga insisted that the girls did their homework and got ready for bed. They reluctantly agreed to go after the current murder was solved. When it was, they kissed their father good night and instinctively gave each of their visitors a kiss on the cheek before trooping off to bed.

There was a pause in the room after they left. Eventually it was Eric who spoke.

"I hope you didn't mind my daughters monopolising your time, gentlemen?"

"Not at all." said Simon. "I haven't had so much fun in years. They are lovely children."

"Cognac?" asked Otto.

"Of course," said Simon as Eric instinctively rose to fetch the decanter and glasses. To his surprise, Otto beat him to it.

"I'll get these, and I insist you join us. I am sure you have many more tales to tell of your exploits in service."

Eric was again surprised but felt strangely relaxed in the company of these two young friends, despite the fact that one was in effect his employer who was here to audit the household accounts.

As the cognac flowed and took effect, the stories flowed more freely from all three men, and when Olga popped her head in the door with a tray of rye bread snacks she could have been mistaken for thinking all three had been at university together. As she left she gave her a husband a stare which meant, 'Don't be long, and don't you dare get too drunk.'

Around midnight, Eric struggled to his feet and informed his visitors that he must go to bed. He thanked them for a very pleasant evening before heading for the door. Otto and Simon stood up and both shook his hand.

"Thank you and good night, Eric," said Simon.

"You're very welcome, Mr Smith. It has been great to think of Scotland again. I have many happy memories from my early days there."

With that he left the younger men together. They were both quite tired too by then, and not a little the worse for wear.

"What a pleasant evening," said Otto.

"Indecd," agreed Simon. "Although it must go down as one of the most bizarre family reunions in the history of the planet."

They both laughed, finished their drinks and headed unsteadily for their rooms. As they went they agreed in slurred tones that Eric was okay, actually - more fun than their supposed fathers had ever been, in fact. It had also been great fun to play Cluedo again, just as they had done with their mothers years before, even if they now knew who had taught them the game. Oh yes, they now had a much better understanding of who had done what, with who and where.

They made their excuses and left after breakfast the next day, and stopped for coffee on the way back to the airport. They had decided on balance that a day's shooting was not what their hangovers needed.

"He's okay, actually," said Simon. "A loveable rogue of course, but I wouldn't mind visiting again sometime."

"I agree," said Otto. "He is certainly more down to earth and human than Kurt. We'll arrange something later in the year."

At the airport they shook hands and separated. Both were lost in their own thoughts.

Chapter Twenty Seven: Billy's Toughest Assignment

After many years of working for Lord Strathbole, Billy Winkman was ready for almost anything. Despite that, he was a little bit surprised one day to be taken out for a drive by his Lordship himself in order to discuss a "particularly thorny problem." His Lordship was usually one to get straight to the point, but on this occasion he seemed to be beating about the bush.

"I've been very pleased with your work, Billy, in all the areas of my affairs where you have proved to be loyal and useful. I appreciate it greatly, along with your discretion of course."

More of the same followed before Billy cut to the chase.

"What do you need me to do?"

"Good man, Billy, I can always rely on you to get to the nub of things. It's like this: there is someone who might cause me considerable problems. So much so, that it would really be better for all concerned, except him of course, if he weren't around at all. If he simply disappeared or dropped down dead it would be something of a blessing."

"Is he a jockey or something?" asked Billy, sounding genuinely concerned for his fellow professionals.

"No, nothing like that. As far as I know he has never ridden in his life. Not horses, anyway. No, he lives and works elsewhere now but he represents a threat to... my family as it were."

Billy was genuinely concerned by a threat to the Strathbole household; indeed he was rather concerned by any threat to his current, rather comfortable set-up.

"Who is he, then?"

"I would be rather grateful if you undertook this little task for me, Billy. Very grateful."

Billy had already made up his mind. He owed a lot to his current employer and didn't want anyone messing up the arrangement he had at the castle. If this person was a threat to his boss, he was a threat to Billy and all that he now enjoyed. It was a step up from his actions so far, but in for a penny, as it were......

"Just point him out to me and consider him history. Don't you worry for a second, Your Lordship. I'll sort him out."

"Good man, Billy. I knew I could rely on you."

Chapter Twenty Eight: Eric Gets an Invitation

Once home in Bavaria, Kurt wasted no time in obtaining details of "The Butler's Ball' and arranging tickets and accommodation for Eric to attend later in the year. He also made sure the documents were purchased and sent on by a junior assistant in one of his many company offices. The assistant had been flattered to be chosen to arrange a trip for a long serving member of the Count's domestic staff and promised to keep it all a secret. What a generous act from the Count, on a mere whim! The assistant decided he had perhaps misjudged the man on the few occasions they had met. Maybe he was not such a cold-hearted bastard after all.

If the assistant was flattered, Eric was completely bemused by the ticket and hotel booking, confirmation of which arrived by post addressed to him. He and his German wife rarely received any mail from outwith the country, never mind an invite to a social event. Of course the invite was only for him on this occasion and he was at first quite reluctant to go. His last memories of Scotland were not the happiest he had, and his wife knew nothing of his wild, younger days. Probably for that reason she was keen that he took up the invitation. She also argued that they got very little from their employer beyond the contracted basics, and if Eric turned down this gift, they might never get anything else from him in the future.

After a brief show of reluctance Eric agreed to his wife's entreaty to go over to Scotland and have a good time. As far as she was concerned her husband was every bit the butler Helmut was and should be taking his rightful place again at the family Schloss. An invite to "The Butler's Ball" from his employer was proof positive that the Count agreed.

"Go there and hold your head high. You are butler to the von Oxburgs, and let everyone there know it!"

She went on to add advice about not drinking too much, wrapping up warmly if he ventured out in Edinburgh's cold winds and ignoring the advances of those loose Scottish women she felt sure would be tempting him at every opportunity. Although he had put on a lot of weight since they had married and had their two daughters, and he now had the red complexion of a regular drinker, she could still remember him as the handsome new butler who arrived from the Schloss and swept her off her feet, quite literally, on his fifth night there.

Eric went from being resigned to having to attend the event to actually looking forward to it rather quickly. He hadn't been back to Scotland since moving to Germany and had only briefly visited London years before with the Count and his wife on a shopping trip one year, shortly before Christmas. The ball offered him the chance of a trip back to his home country. He had no living family there as far as he was aware but missed some of the simple pleasures he had had to give up by moving to Germany. Traditional Scottish beer was quite different from the German ales he found locally and he was attracted by the chance of sampling some again. A full cooked breakfast with not a single healthy option on the plate was another thing which had become only a distant memory, especially after he married his wife.

When the day arrived for him to travel to Scotland he kissed his wife goodbye at the station and took a train to Mulhouse airport with something of a spring in his step. He was now completely looking forward to a rare weekend of freedom; visiting his old haunts in Edinburgh was a bonus but just a weekend away from the mundane routine of domestic life was attractive in itself.

He arrived at the airport quite early and watched people going by as he sipped a coffee, realising how remote the house in Alsace really was, and how much of the world he had never seen or experienced. As a group of air stewardesses walked past him, each trailing the obligatory flight case behind them, an old familiar urge also reawakened. He was, of course, happily married now with two beautiful daughters that he adored, but although he would never actively try to cheat on his wife the trip to Edinburgh might just provide a romantic opportunity too.

His otherwise contented family life was rather tame compared to his younger days in the company of the many ladies who found his looks and bearing irresistible.

Chapter Twenty Nine: Billy Meets Eric

The week before Eric arrived at the Grand Pacific Hotel for the Butler's Ball, Billy Winkman returned to his cottage to find an unmarked envelop had been pushed through his letterbox. Inside he found a photograph of a middle aged man in butler's livery, a scrap of paper with the words "Eric Ramsay, Grand Pacific Hotel room 202" along with the dates of two nights, a week later, and the time of a flight arriving at Edinburgh airport. In addition was a bundle of used notes totalling £1000.

"I don't mind if I do, Your Lordship," said Billy before adding. "Although you really didn't have to."

He pocketed the money and the photograph before memorising the dates and burning the slip of paper. He knew the hotel well enough from a boxing tournament he had taken part in years before. It had been a grand affair in the ballroom of the hotel with men in evening jackets sitting at tables, baying for blood during each fight. Beside most of them sat ladies in formal dresses who either shouted for blood too or hid their eyes during the bouts.

Billy had been robbed of victory that night as usual, losing on points to a young lad from Paisley. At least there was the subsequent consolation of watching the lad rise through the ranks and have a short and unsuccessful crack at a world title some years later.

The following week Billy positioned himself opposite the main entrance to the hotel and waited. After two hours of waiting he was rewarded with a view of Eric Ramsay's arrival.

Eric had arrived mid-afternoon and Billy had rightly judged that he would take a wander round Edinburgh before dinner. When Eric left the hotel through the main entrance an hour or so later Billy followed him.

Eric Ramsay seemed to know his way around Edinburgh and headed for a bar in Rose Street. Billy followed him inside and stood beside him to order a drink. When both men had a drink and as they were both on their own they inevitably got talking. Eric explained why he was in Edinburgh and Billy made up a story of working on a building project over the weekend and planning to hit the town on the Friday and Saturday nights, hopefully to pick up some women in bars and clubs which he knew.

Eric's interest was gained and after a few more drinks, the men agreed to meet up after the dinner on the first night of Eric's convention and to hit the town together. It was further agreed that they would meet in Eric's room and have a large dram before heading out. Eric checked his watch and said he'd better head back. They shook hands and bid a farewell till the following night.

As he was leaving Eric said, "Not a word of this to anyone mind. What happens in Edinburgh, stays in Edinburgh."

Billy smiled and nodded. "I couldn't have put it better myself," he whispered under his breath as Eric left.

Chapter Thirty: One Double Room

The acts for the Butlers' Ball were required to arrive two days before the event for rehearsals and so Lola and George walked into the foyer of the Grand Pacific late in the morning of the appointed day, having been dropped off by a rather concerned Janine. She was happy enough regarding Lola's knife-throwing skills, but did not fully trust her left alone with George. Her disapproval was tempered by the fact that it had all been her idea for George to take part. Admittedly, she had been rather drunk when she suggested it, and had also assumed that Lola would only need George for auditions and rehearsals until she persuaded someone else to take his place. Now she found herself driving her boyfriend to a hotel for the weekend with someone whose favourite pastime seemed to be taking her clothes off at the first opportunity. She had hinted at her concerns to George who had assured her that he would never dream of taking advantage of the situation. That may be true, she thought, but she had no such confidence in Lola.

Lola and George walked up to the reception desk and found a rather flustered night manager still on duty. His replacement had been drafted into the preparations for the weekend's event and there was no immediate prospect of him getting home for a much needed rest. As a result his patience was wafer thin.

"We are here for the ball. We are Les Cortez," announced Lola rather grandly.

The night manager was unimpressed. He had already checked in a tightrope walker, four dwarves who were still dressed as clowns to save their luggage requirements and a very tall American woman who was more concerned about her lions and tigers which were arriving simultaneously at the goods entrance than she was about her own room.

"Room 407," he said mechanically and handed them a form to sign and a card key for the door.

"And my room…?" asked George.

"Who are you?"

"I'm George Milne," said George Milne.

The night manager looked at him and then at Lola.

"I assumed you were the other Cortez."

"I am but we will need separate rooms. We are an act but not an item."

The manager looked at him again, wondering whether or not to be polite and show any sympathy. On balance he must have given up.

"Tough. You are booked into room 407 as Les Cortez. There are no other rooms left so you will have to share. Whatever acts you perform or whether you become an item or not is up to you. One of you sign here please."

George was about to argue further for a separate room but Lola told him not to bother and signed for the room and key.

As they walked away towards the lift George began to complain, conscious of a slight feeling of concern beginning in his stomach.

"What will Janine say about us sharing a room?"

"If you are foolish enough to tell her, quite a bit, I imagine. On the other hand I am sure I can resist your charms, and if nothing happens you have nothing to tell her about; do you?"

George paused for a moment or two while they waited for the lift and had to admit she had a point. There was no immediate need to tell Janine. To do that would jeopardise their appearance on the Saturday night. If that didn't happen Lola wouldn't get her fee and might not move out and begin her world tour, which was Janine's main priority. In that way he couldn't possibly mess things up now. If he did it would somehow be unfair on Janine. The best and most faithful thing he could do as her boyfriend was to share a room with Lola and say no more about it, even if she stripped naked.

The lift arrived, four tiny clowns got out and Lola and George got in. They didn't speak as the lift went up to their floor. When they opened the door of the room they realised it must be one of the smallest in the building, possibly former staff accommodation. A double bed had been squeezed in along with the standard fittings of bedside tables, lamps, a TV and a trouser press. The room was ensuite, having a bathroom half the size of the bedroom with a shower but no bath.

Lola trailed her flight case into the room and threw herself down on the bed which she immediately declared was perfectly acceptable. George followed her in with slight hesitation, but he had already decided to do the right thing by Janine and wasn't going to back out now. He had convinced himself that sharing this tiny bedroom with Lola for three nights was what Janine would want him to do, although he decided he wouldn't phone her to double check.

Their booking for the show also required them to check in with the hotel manager who was going to be acting as master of ceremonies, and they were to do this in costume.

"Right then, let's get changed," said Lola as she hoisted her dress over her head and reached for her flight case.

"I suppose we should," agreed George reaching for his battered old case without taking his eyes off Lola.

Twenty minutes after they had left it they re-entered the lift, making way for the returning clowns before they did so. Again they said nothing as the lift descended to the ground floor. As the doors opened, an impossibly tall lady walked in without giving them the chance to get out first. The woman was wearing what looked like a traditional ringmaster's costume but with the trousers cut away and sequined tights on her legs. Part of her height at least was due to a pair of eight inch heeled boots, but she would have appeared very tall whatever.

"Why does no one in this hotel understand tigers? Of course they'll bite you if you go too close. I never have this problem in Vegas," she said to nobody in particular.

George wondered who had been bitten. The tiny clowns were no smaller than they had been on their downward journey.

They followed the signs to the Grand Ballroom and found it a hive of activity. Tables were being set out around the hall and extra spotlights fitted to the ceiling. Signs warning people not to walk under the mobile scaffolding were being ignored by all. In the centre of the room a man in harlequin lounge slacks and cut-away tee shirt was trying to set up two posts which had a thin wire strung loosely between them. In the middle of the sea of confusion was a very calm looking man also dressed as a ringmaster but with a complete pair of trousers rather than tights and a clip board in his hand. He noticed Lola and George arrive and signalled for them to come over.

After quickly looking them up and down he asked, "Les Cortez or The Davidson Plate Spinners?"

"Les Cortez," said Lola in her rather grand way, as if she already had an audience.

The man ticked them off his list before asking in a friendly way: "Everything alright with your room?"

George was about to revisit the issue of separate rooms when Lola confirmed the room was "adequate", her use of the word suggesting that she was used to better but would make do just this once.

"Good. Costumes look fine. We start rehearsals today after lunch; can you be here ready to perform at 1.30, please? You haven't seen four small clowns, have you?"

George confirmed that the clowns had just passed them on the fourth floor, presumably heading back to their rooms.

"Bloody clowns," said the ringmaster. "They still haven't reported to me yet. If you see them could you ask them to appear here before lunch. I've tried to phone their room but there's no reply."

Lola and George nodded and then headed slowly towards the door again. As they walked they watched the frenetic activity in the ballroom and both felt the first pangs of nervousness. As they reached the lift it opened and the clowns again walked out, this time accompanied by a member of staff. The five of them were followed out of the lift by the American lion tamer who now had a large whip in her hand and looked for all the world as if she was herding the clowns towards the ballroom.

Back at the room Lola took the opportunity of removing her dress and flopping down on the bed.

"We have an hour and a half to relax before we start rehearsals. I'm going to have forty winks and I suggest you do the same."

George was not particularly tired but as he was the junior partner in the act and all this show business stuff was new to him he decided to comply, and slowly lay down on the bed beside Lola's now naked body. As his head hit the pillow his bow-tie shot off and he prayed that there were no hidden cameras in the room. His confidence in Janine's understanding was waning more than a little and the sight of Lola's body beside him was testing his resolve.

George hadn't expected to sleep but found that he was woken by the alarm on the room phone which Lola had taken the precaution of setting before collapsing on the bed. The clock on the television control box indicated that they had fifteen minutes to get ready and return to the ballroom so they both rose quickly, used the toilet in turns and got fully dressed.

They found that the lift arrived empty for a change and made their way quickly to the stage area, wondering if they were in fact late. They needn't have worried as they were the first to turn up. Indeed it transpired that the Davidson Plate Spinning act had still to check into the hotel. The ringmaster looked delighted that Les Cortez had appeared and asked if they would mind going first, even though on the night they would appear just before the lion tamer provided a spectacular finale.

"Not at all," said Lola catching George out with her confidence and he quickly found himself behind the now closed curtains trying hard to focus on his part in the act rather than the recent sight of Lola sleeping.

Almost immediately the curtains opened again and he walked to the centre of the stage carrying the sparking knives. He bowed, waved for Lola to join him, which she did, and they then paused briefly before George handed over the knives and took his place beside the target wheel which had been delivered the day before and was now set up ready to use.

There was a childish giggle from the manager dressed as a ringmaster, who loved the circus, and Les Cortez ran through the rest of their act. At the end the ring master clapped briefly but enthusiastically, and gave them the thumbs up.

"Excellent," he said. "We are still rounding up some of the other acts and there is a question mark over health and safety regarding the tigers after this morning's little incident, but at least I know you guys are good to go. We'll run through the whole thing in order this evening, but you can rest up till seven tonight if you like. Obviously you are welcome to stay and watch the other acts if you prefer; I know I would."

Lola declined on their behalf and George found himself relieved. He was still a bit unwell from the spinning wheel part of the act, and also hungry from starving himself before rehearsals. This conflict resolved itself as they passed the restaurant and he knew he had to eat. When he suggested a late lunch Lola shrugged and followed him into the table. George had never seen her hungry and although she did eat it seemed to be an optional activity for her; it never took the place of living.

After a large lunch and a few drinks, George and Lola headed back to the room, passing nobody on the way, and both lay down on the bed for an afternoon nap as if they were an elderly couple.

Still too full for an evening meal, and mindful of George's habit of throwing up after spinning on the wheel, they ate nothing else before again making their way to the stage for the designated start time of seven. The room itself had been transformed. In the centre was a large steel cage with strong-looking, low stands for the lions and tigers. In the centre of it a high-wire had been erected. Around the outside of the cage, tables had been set up to seat several hundred people, with candelabra and silverware on every one. The stage had a full array of extra lights and three large men in teeshirts and tracksuits were discussing the movement of equipment needed between acts.

The other transformation was in the state of the ringmaster who was no longer the calm and childlike circus fan he had been earlier. He was having a heated discussion with someone via his mobile phone as Lola and George arrived.

"No they fucking can't use our plates. If their carrier smashed theirs they need to buy more or pull out. You tell Davidson that and tell him he'd better appear here in the next ten minutes with something entertaining or he's out. Oh and find those fucking dwarves. If they've gone to the bar again refuse them service for the remainder of their stay." There was a pause. "I don't know; ask them for proof of age."

With that the ringmaster turned to Les Cortez and tried to smile a reassuring smile.

"Just the usual teething problems. You must see it all the time?"

"Not really," said Lola unsympathetically.

The ringmaster tried the smile again, then gave up and asked the tightrope walker, now dressed as Charlie Chaplin, to be ready to start his act in ten minutes if the clowns hadn't appeared to open the show.

The clowns didn't appear to open the show, so the tightrope walker started things off with a passable impression of Chaplin walking with his cane towards the high-wire. Things might have gone better for him if the floor of the cage hadn't had huge dollops of Big Cat droppings dotted around it. Ever the pro, the high-wire performer built this into his act as he made his way towards the ladder beside one of the supports, avoiding the poo with exaggerated movements. Unfortunately as he reached the ladder he misjudged an unnecessarily large step and put his foot into one of the piles.

"Shit," he said briefly out of character before re-entering the world of silent entertainment and climbing up to the wire. By this time though, one of his special shoes was slippy with an unpleasant coating and he kept losing his footing. He continued for a few minutes before giving up, neatly swinging down from the wire and approaching the ringmaster to complain bitterly about the state of his approach surface.

"I can't be expected to perform on the wire if I have to walk through a pet toilet to get there. You'll have to do something about the mess."

An exasperated ringmaster looked round at the lion tamer who was sprawled across a chair near the stage.

"Can't you stop them pooing in the cage?" he asked her.

"They are wild animals. You house train them," she replied without any obvious interest and returned to her day dreams of the glory days in Las Vegas.

"That's not very helpful really," he replied. "Come and have a look at the mess just from your afternoon rehearsal."

The tall American rose to her feet and walked over to stand beside him. In their almost identical outfits she looked for all the world like a big sister about to take a considerably younger brother trick or treating at Halloween. She stared at the droppings in the cage.

"That is what they do I am afraid. There isn't normally a support act inside the cage too. Can't the tightrope walker use the stage like everybody else?"

"The wire doesn't fit," shouted the wire-walker, annoyed at being referred to as a support act.

"Then you will have to clean up before you go on," said the lion tamer before returning to her seat.

"I'm not clearing anybody else's shit from anywhere. You get a bucket or put nappies on your pussy cats," the walker shouted after her.

The ringmaster signalled to the men in tee-shirts and tracksuit bottoms to come over and after a lengthy discussion which seemed to centre round an additional payment it was agreed they would clean the floor after each appearance by the big cats.

The ringmaster's phone rang and he had a brief heated conversation with the person at the other end. He looked round at all the acts, which now included the Davidson Plate Spinners, and advised they would try the show again from the beginning. The tightrope walker groaned and started to change his shoes but noticed the props men were now cleaning the floor of the cage. He at least felt vindicated.

The ringmaster put the phone to his ear again and said: "Send in the clowns."

The plan had been for the clowns to appear from all four doors simultaneously accompanied by suitable circus music and interact with members of the audience before commencing their own act together inside the cage. Unfortunately they were proving harder to control than the lions and tigers and all appeared from the door nearest the bar with a member of security behind them.

Sober, their clowning around might have been funny but drunk and uncoordinated it merged tragedy and farce in equal measures. Their attempts at both juggling and tumbling were a disaster and eventually the ringmaster called a halt.

He went over to the leader of the troupe and had a stern word with him about professionalism. Had it been in Hungarian it might have hit home. As it was, though, the tone had sufficient effect that the clowns gathered together, spoke briefly amongst themselves before the leader apologised and they headed, contritely, for an early night. The member of security was dispatched to make sure they did exactly that.

Thereafter the rehearsal ran its course with the Davidsons' being the weakest link with only four plates to use in their act but everyone else performing well. Lola and George went through their routine in a suitably professional manner and took a bow before the finale got under way.

The lights dimmed, a recorded drum roll was played through the PA system and a spotlight picked out two lions and two tigers which made their way through the tunnel from the stage and into the cage. Proud of their own acts as they were, the rest of the cast had to admit it was an impressive sight. It became even more impressive when the tall American lion tamer entered the cage via a double door near the stage end and cracked her whip. At first the animals made a play of being fierce and rebellious but after a further few cracks of the whip, they fell into line and went through an act consisting of various acrobatics including literally jumping through hoops for their mistress. In the final part of her act, one of the lions steadfastly refused to close its jaws round the lion tamer's head despite the fact that it was placed between them. With a final crack of the whip the beasts headed back out of the cage and their owner took a bow. There was a spontaneous round of applause from those watching and she took another bow.

"Bravo," shouted the ringmaster having regained to his boyish enthusiasm from the afternoon. "Thank you everybody. Be here ready to go tomorrow at nine please. I'll sort the clowns out by then so that we can have a full run through."

George and Lola headed for the bar as the ringmaster engaged the Davidsons in an earnest discussion about plates.

Chapter Thirty One: A few Drinks and Then to Bed

The bar of the Grand Pacific Hotel had seen some strange gatherings over the years, but the scene during the first evening of rehearsals may have set new levels. At the bar itself, a lady in a sequined leotard with feathers in her hair was in deep conversation with an older man who, from a distance, looked like a clown. At the side of the woman's barstool were propped a bundle of long sparkling knives. Beside them at the bar were two female Chinese acrobats in snakeskin leotards sipping on green tea. Next to them were three broad shouldered men in tracksuit bottoms and tee-shirts who were desperately trying to include either the Chinese acrobats or the lady with the feathers in their increasingly boisterous conversation. At the far end of the bar a very tall lady in a ring master's costume was having a heated argument with Charlie Chaplin, which appeared to be refereed by her little brother. Two men on unicycles were juggling their empty shots glasses for a bet they had accepted from three men in business suits who hadn't even thought about the circus for years before that night. Other groups of business people and a few couples were dotted around the tables in the bar watching everything going on as if the entertainment had been arranged for their enjoyment.

As a little comic relief from the tableau ranged around the bar itself, every hour or so four tiny clowns would enter the bar from different directions and try to buy drinks only to be refused by the bar-staff as if they were children and then be escorted from the premises by a security guard. Against this backdrop, the married couple in sequined jumpsuits twirling and occasionally breaking china plates in a corner booth went largely unnoticed.

George and Lola were feeling rather pleased with themselves. At each rehearsal their act had gone well, and while it may have lacked the impact of the Big Cats in the finale, it was still an entertaining penultimate act in the show. Their efforts had been rewarded with enthusiasm by the master of ceremonies who had also commented a few times that at least he could rely on one act being fully prepared.

"Should I take longer to hand over the knives and maybe get a bigger laugh?" asked George in high spirits.

"No, the timing is perfect as it is," replied Lola who was also loving the whole atmosphere.

"What about the 'who you?' bit of miming I do?"

"No, it's good the way you have been doing it. Any more and it will look as if you are trying to compete with Charlie Chaplin over there, and in fairness, he has the edge."

"This is fun though," said George. "I didn't even feel sick the last time I got off the wheel. Another drink?"

"Why not, though you'd better not have too many if we are on at nine tomorrow morning; another Martini and Gin. No lemonade this time," replied Lola, now fully relaxed. As she said it she leaned over and squeezed George's knee before whispering in his ear, "Thank you."

The drinks arrived and they went back to discussing the finer points of the act, for want of a better topic of conversation.

As the evening wore on, the bar slowly but surely emptied. Even the clowns stopped re-appearing and shortly after midnight Lola and George headed for their room; George staggering slightly but Lola walking beside him as steady as a rock and providing support when necessary. Again they had the lift to themselves and made their way to room 407. Once there, George let Lola use the bathroom first and was no longer surprised when she reappeared naked and climbed into bed with a yawn. He used the bathroom next, brushing his teeth thoroughly before putting on the new pyjamas Janine had packed for him and then returning to the bedroom. Lola was sound asleep and George climbed gently into his side of the bed and soon, drifted into a deep sleep.

The clock suggested it was half past two when George woke to find hands gently caressing his stomach and his legs. At first he thought Lola was still asleep and was having a dream, but as her expert hands began to explore other areas of his anatomy he realised her movements were those of a fully conscious woman. He wasn't sure what to do and was about to object when Lola put a finger to his lips before climbing on top of him and dispelling any thoughts of sleep for the next hour or so.

In the morning when he was awoken by the sounds of singing coming from the shower, he took a while to work out where he was. Slowly but surely, though, he pieced together where he was, who was singing and everything which had happened the night before.

"Bugger!" he said quietly to himself, feeling a slight hangover setting in.

Chapter Thirty Two: Fear and Loathing in Edinburgh

George had telephoned Janine after the first run through the act and had re-assured her that it had gone well, as indeed it had. He had answered her questions honestly regarding his room being small but comfortable and having a shower but no bath. He had described the late lunch in detail and confirmed that Lola was happy with her room too, which was also small and had a shower but no bath. He decided that the minor detail of it being the same room in each case was not relevant and as Janine never asked, he had no reason to tell her. Also it never came up in conversation that they would have to spend three nights sharing the same bed. Again, Janine never asked him if they would have to, so he never had to tell her. He finished the call with a fairly clear conscience. The same could not be said about the way he started the next day. His conscience was anything but clear by then. Admittedly he had gone to bed beside a sleeping, if naked, Lola with the intention of enjoying nothing more than a good night's sleep. The fact that it had been interrupted by Lola's sexual desires was hardly his fault; he was sure Janine would agree with that much at least. He tried to convince himself that he had somehow been used against his will, but having said nothing remotely close to "please stop that", he struggled.

He raised his concerns at the breakfast table with Lola who seemed to be in fine form.

"Forget it, George. It was just one of those things. You had nothing to do with it, really," she assured him.

"But I was rather involved, don't you think?"

"Only just, George. Janine would understand, trust me. It's a woman thing."

George remained unconvinced but returned to his light breakfast, conscious of the fact that he would be spinning round on the large wheel in under an hour.

He was still obviously dwelling on what had happened when they went on stage as he lacked his usual commitment to the act and even dropped the knives as he handed them to Lola. She recovered them quickly but could see that his mind was on the events of the night before rather than the job in hand. The afternoon rehearsal was little better and she resolved that something had to be done.

"George, are you still worrying about last night?" she asked as they went for a quick nap in their room between afternoon rehearsals.

"Well, a bit - yes," admitted George. "I am worried what Janine would say if she found out. I don't think she would be as understanding as you seem to think."

"You have a nap, George, and I will sort everything out."

George was tired and found himself drifting off into a deep sleep.

He awoke to hear Lola on the telephone.

"I wouldn't read too much into it, darling. After all a cock is just a cock."

There was a pause as whoever was at the other end of the call spoke loudly for some time. George tried to make out what was being said and who it was but could not. He was drifting over to sleep again when Lola spoke again.

"Well, you must do what you think best. If you must; you must."

With that Lola put the phone down and turned to George, realising he was awake.

"Who was that?" he said sleepily.

"Janine. I thought I'd better let her know what happened so that you could relax and concentrate on the act."

"What?" shouted George, bouncing out of bed. "You told her we were sharing a room and... and ... well ... last night's thing?"

"Yes, I thought it best. Clear the air and clear your mind."

"And was she as understanding as you expected?"

"Strangely enough, no. She insists on coming up to Edinburgh to give you a piece of her mind. Why she wants to do that I have no idea. I assured her that I could talk things through with you but nothing would do except drive up here and, no doubt, shout at you till she's hoarse. I just hope she doesn't interrupt rehearsals."

All of a sudden George needed to use the toilet. This had become a nightmare. Lola had probably just ruined everything he and Janine had together, and worse still, he had to listen to Janine shout the details of what had gone wrong at him. Today. He was sure that pointing out to her that his taking part in the act was her idea wouldn't get him very far.

'Bugger!' he thought to himself as he sat on the toilet, resigned to the inevitable. Mind you, after Glenda and her mother, perhaps it wouldn't be too bad.

But he was wrong.

Chapter Thirty Three: Circus Interruptus

As he and Lola made their way to the ballroom for the second rehearsal of the afternoon, he found himself trying to calculate how long it would take Janine to drive to the hotel and find him. He had estimated that he had about an hour and a half but as events turned out, he had been over-optimistic by about twenty minutes. Janine arrived in the ballroom as Les Cortez took to the stage. She saw George appear on stage and start his mime act. Due to the spotlights, he could not see her and was still hoping to complete the rehearsal and hide before she arrived. As he turned to hand the knives to Lola he found Janine standing there instead.

"Just what I need, George Milne: knives," she said as she took them from his shaking hand.

Lola entered from stage left and tried to calm the situation.

"You shouldn't over-react, Janine; I just needed a man, and George was the first one that came to hand, as it were," she said calmly.

"You keep your hands to yourself, I've a good mind to use these knives on you, you little tart. Get your own man for once," Janine shouted back, momentarily distracted from her desire to kill George.

The ringmaster had been expecting to see the standard knife throwing act and had hoped it would go better than the previous run-throughs that day. Instead he saw a woman he did not recognise take the knives and threaten to kill both Les Cortez in turn. Unfazed after years in the hospitality industry he called for security on his house mobile and signalled for the props men to separate the three warring factions on the stage.

"I can explain," said George unconvincingly, well aware that he could think of no reasonable explanation likely to placate Janine.

"Don't bloody bother," shouted Janine as she separated one of the knives from the bundle.

George was relieved to see one of the props men arrive on stage beside Janine and start to attempt to take the knives away from her. After a struggle he managed, and two of his colleagues took his place as he carried the knives to a neutral corner.

"I thought you were different, George Milne; a bit odd admittedly, but different. But you are just like all the other men I have ever met," screamed Janine.

"I told you," said Lola. "A cock is a cock."

"That's not what I meant you half-Spanish bint. Don't expect me to be there when you get home, you bastard. We are finished, George Milne. Finished."

The two props men had handed restraint duties on Janine over to the security staff who by then had arrived on stage, and they led her towards the front door with firm but professional skill. As she disappeared from view, still shouting at George and Lola, the lion tamer started clapping.

"Now that is what I call entertainment," she said to nobody in particular.

The ringmaster gave her a stare which suggested her comments were not helpful, before turning back to George and Lola.

"We will take a few minutes' break and then let me know if you are ready and indeed willing to continue."

There was a groan from the other acts and an assistant manager quickly stopped the clowns from heading for the bar. On the stage George stood motionless. He couldn't believe that helping Lola with her stupid act had led to him losing Janine. On reflection he was fairly sure that was what had just happened. She clearly meant that she would not be there when he got back home.

Lola came over to where he was standing and put her hand on his back.

"I am sorry, George, I can't help feeling somehow responsible for what happened there."

George stared at her.

"You are entirely responsible for what happened there," he said.

"Oh I don't know. It takes two to tango. Anyway, the show must go on. Try to make the mime a bit more convincing this time round. Matthew," she shouted at the ringmaster. "Ready when you are!"

George went through the motions of participating in the act and then went straight to the room to lie down as soon as he was untied from the wheel. He wasn't tired anymore; he was angry: Angry at Lola, angry at himself and even a little bit angry at Janine for talking him into taking part in the act in the first place. Why couldn't people just let things stay the same? He lay down on the bed but this time didn't sleep.

Chapter Thirty Four: Lola meets Hamish

While George headed for the room, a rather dejected figure, Lola made her way to the bar, still in her leotard and feather headdress. It had been unpleasant she thought, but, on balance, "job done!" Her aim had been slightly off during the spinning wheel finale and she had realised her hands were shaking slightly. There was no quicker way of solving that particular problem than by having a few drinks.

As she entered the bar she noticed a well-dressed and distinguished looking man eye her up and down. He obviously liked what he saw and walked over to where she was standing before she had time to order a drink for herself.

"I hope you don't mind me being a bit old-fashioned," said Hamish Strathbole, "But I hate to see a lady drink on her own, in a public bar. May I buy you a drink? or are you expecting company, in which case I do apologise for being so forward."

Lola was a sucker for a rich man with manners who appeared to be alone, and so she accepted the offer of a drink. When her Martini, gin and lemonade arrived she raised it and toasted his generosity.

"Cheers," she said.

"Bottoms up," Hamish replied with the most obvious leer Lola had ever seen.

"Who knows? The night is yet young," she replied with a giggle.

"I guess you are part of the floor show for tomorrow night, going by your delightfully skimpy costume. What is your particular act?"

"I am part of the knife throwing act, though I won't tell you any more in case I spoil the impact. Are you here for The Butler's Ball? You don't look like a butler to me."

"I apologise for not introducing myself earlier. I am Hamish Strathbole, Lord Strathbole, and I am the Honorary President of The British Society of Gentlemen's Gentlemen, many of whom have worked for me over the years."

"It's a pleasure and an honour," said Lola, suddenly warming to her new acquaintance. "What should I call you? Lord Strathbole?"

"Please call me Hamish. All my friends do."

Chapter Thirty Five: Dress Rehearsal

Lola appeared for the dress rehearsal that evening directly from the bar. She walked in a very straight line and her hands were no longer shaking. Her evening meal consisted of three martinis, gin and lemonade, undiluted by food. George dutifully appeared from the room, having shared the lift with the clowns. When the ringmaster judged that everyone was ready and security were in place, he began his routine as if all the seats were full. The clowns appeared on cue and played to the occasional member of staff sat at a table for the purpose.

One act followed another and things went like clockwork. George felt obliged to rise to the occasion and put on a flawless performance. The lions and tigers seemed to sense the importance of a dress rehearsal and roared louder and looked wilder than they had before. When the show was over the ringmaster gave everyone an enthusiastic round of applause and asked them to be on time for the main event the following night. Everyone trooped to the bar in good spirits, except Lola, who trooped to the lift and made her way to Lord Strathbole's suite in equally good mood. George found himself alone at the bar on something of a low. He had one drink and then, finding himself still alone, headed for the room and a bath followed by an early night. He was tired and needed some rest. He had no great hope of being woken during the night this time round as Lola had headed off after telling him not to wait up.

Chapter Thirty Six: Dinner and a Show

The following day dragged on for all the acts involved in the evening's entertainment, but for nobody more so than George. He woke up in the morning in an empty bed and quickly remembered the events from the previous two days. The memories did little to encourage him to bounce out of bed and seize the day.

He lay there wondering how on earth he had got involved with Lola Cortez and her circus act. Life had been just fine till she appeared on the scene. Now he had the prospect of returning to an empty house when the show was finished and he found himself more than a little depressed at the prospect.

Admittedly life would be quiet and peaceful again but he knew he would miss the company and intimacy of Janine's presence. No amount of tea and chocolate biscuits could make up for that.

He also had to go through a performance tonight in front of several hundred people supporting the ambitions of the woman who had caused all the problems with Janine in the first place; a woman who didn't even have the decency to sleep with him two nights in a row before finding a new attraction elsewhere.

Eventually he dragged himself out of bed and showered. He made a cup of coffee using the kettle in the room and ate both the speculus biscuits, then he dressed in his casual clothes and went down to breakfast. He found himself to be the only circus act there, and after eating a full fry up without any enthusiasm he left the hotel and went for a long walk round Edinburgh.

After several hours of walking and a coffee in Waverley Station which he made last an hour and a half, he returned to his hotel room to find Lola naked and asleep on the bed. Still low but by now quite tired, he took his own clothes off and lay down beside her, having first checked that the alarm was set to wake them in plenty of time for the actual performance that evening.

At the appointed hour they awoke and showered and dressed, George saying nothing and Lola chatting away about touring Europe as if nothing of note had happened.

By then George had resolved to perform his part in the act as well as he could, return home alone and get back to the quiet life he had previously enjoyed there. He would miss Janine, he knew, and it would be a lonely existence in some people's eyes, but there were far worse things than being alone.

The hotel had filled up during the day with butlers and salesmen from the related industries and all circus acts had to use the rear staff stairway to get to the ballroom, as much out of sheer practicality as to keep the surprise for the show itself.

George and Lola made their way to the dressing area to the rear of the stage and found, to George's surprise, that all the acts were already there, sober and dressed to impress. The ringmaster was the only one showing any nerves as the professionals went through their final preparations.

After dinner had been served and cleared, the lights dimmed, a drumroll sounded over the tannoy and the ringmaster burst through the curtains to a round of applause. Despite all the teething problems at rehearsals, the show flowed seamlessly through the acts in turn. George and Lola went down extremely well with the audience and the Grand Finale had the desired impact too. Even the clowns were bang on with their timing and had the audience in fits as they tumbled and improvised throughout the evening

When all the acts had taken a final bow and the curtains closed for the last time, Lola turned to George and gave him a huge hug.

"Thank you, George. Thank you for everything you have done for me."

Then she kissed him and, still high on adrenaline, they headed for the bar with anything but sleep on their minds.

As they did so they failed to see a small figure in overalls pass them on his way to the rear stairwell via the stage area. As the figure passed the stage, he stopped and looked at the apparatus stored at the sides. In particular, the 12 spangled knives leaning against a large wheel-like device caught his eye and he walked over to them. After checking that nobody was looking, he took one of the knives and hid it inside the overalls before continuing to the stairs and making his way to the bedrooms above.

Chapter Thirty Seven: Murder at the Butlers' Convention

Inspector Jimmy Bell liked murder in a professional way. It was the ultimate crime which detectives, like himself, had to solve. He had seen his fair share of corpses in his time in the west coast of Scotland and Lanarkshire. He had gained promotion on the strength of solving a tidal wave of murders focussed round the late, unlamented Frankie Cook. As a Detective Inspector in Edinburgh it gave him an air of credibility which many of his colleagues lacked. Yes, murder was the life blood of his profession. He just didn't like murder on his own patch. That was quite different. It required him to solve it and placed pressures on his time. It threatened his hard-won reputation. In short it meant he had to work, and work hard under the close scrutiny of both the press and his superiors.

When the call came in that a guest had been found stabbed to death at the Grand Pacific Hotel in the city centre it ruined his evening. It had taken the edge off the guest's evening too, he had to admit, but at least for him the inconvenience had now ended. For Jimmy it had just begun. The press heard about it shortly afterwards. They would have run with the story anyway, but when they discovered that the dead man was a butler attending a Butlers Convention they suspected Christmas had come early. Jimmy's phone started ringing soon after that as every press contact he had ever sought a favour from or vice versa tried to get the inside story.

By the time he headed for the hotel he was ready to kill the next person who asked him if he thought the butler did it.

Jimmy arrived at room 202 with his assistant, Det Sgt Janice Young, and they made their way past the scene of crime team, nodding at the uniformed constable as they passed. The victim lay on the floor near the window with a knife in his back; no ordinary knife either. It was about 18 inches long with a spangle of pink sequins inlaid on the handle. The blade was broad and heavy and obviously sharp from the depth of penetration into the corpse. For all the world, it looked to Jimmy like the kind of throwing-knife circus acts used. The body had grey receding hair swept back to hide the thinning area. He had once been quite tall by the look of him.

Jimmy's first thought was some ritualistic killing. He had watched a film once where a young Sherlock Holmes had solved the mystery of an Eastern cult transported to Victorian London who killed their sacrificial victims with similar knives. Admittedly the cult used curved knives, but the similarity was striking.

Jimmy's mood had improved now that he was at the scene of the crime. There was a certain seriousness in the professional way everyone went about their own job. Since his arrival at the hotel nobody had made any quips about the butler doing it. The management of the hotel had been traumatised by a brutal murder on their premises. Their bosses in the States had been traumatised by the possible effect on future bookings, and indeed the likely dip in takings during the current weekend, which they had expected to be a bumper event.

Jimmy's expression had ruled out any humorous comments from the uniformed police who had secured the crime scene. There was no attempt at humour, either, from the scene-of-crime team who had got to work as soon as the body was discovered and declared officially dead. Mind you, thought Jimmy, considering the individuals concerned, they seemed to be devoid of humour at all times anyway.

He turned to the senior figure in the team and asked, "What have you got for me?"

"Deceased male, one Eric Ramsay, age 62, professional butler. Cause of death, unofficially, stab wound to the back causing perforation of several arteries in the heart. Death almost immediate. Weapon, large throwing-style knife. Two sets of prints on the knife; one male one female."

"Anything else you can speculate at the moment?" asked Jimmy.

The head of the scene-of-crime team, Ruth Swanson, frowned, as if her professional integrity had been insulted. "I am not employed to speculate. I am employed to establish facts; thereafter it is over to you to speculate."

"I know, I know," said Jimmy impatiently. "Just predict what I might speculate when I get your report. It could save some time."

"You might be led to speculate that the blow was from behind the victim, there is no evidence of a struggle, and therefore he knew his assailant and had turned away, perhaps to the bottle of whisky over there to pour two drinks, feeling under no threat. There are two glasses on the floor. Both have traces of whisky in them and his finger prints. There is also a large amount of the spirit on the carpet next to the body."

Jimmy nodded, aware of the rules of this game with Ruth. She would speculate as well as the next person; just don't quote her on anything but the facts.

"It looks like a throwing-knife. Was it thrown or used to stab the victim?" Jimmy asked, hoping for facts but ready to accept speculation. In the end he got neither.

"We won't know one way or the other till the autopsy." Ruth shrugged her shoulders suggesting no great hurry on her part and she returned to her little evidence bags and photographer assistant.

"If it was thrown it would have to have been by someone who knew what they were doing," Jimmy said to DS Young. "My gut feeling is that the person used it to stab him, but hopefully the autopsy can confirm that asap."

The two spent another minute or so looking round the murder scene, and decided there was nothing more to be gained from it at that time. Instead, Jimmy decided they would make their way back to the entrance and see how the incident team were getting on with the lists of staff and guests.

They walked the short distance from the room to the lift and again nodded to the uniformed officer on duty. If the gesture signified anything, it signified that Jimmy and Janice were glad they were out of that lark and that the bored uniformed officer wished he were too. At least he was in out of the rain for a change and safe on duty here till his shift finished. How many free cups of coffee and cakes could be blagged in a classy hotel, they all wondered.

Inside the lift, Jimmy started voicing his thoughts again, hoping for some kind of reassurance from his junior colleague.

"I want a complete check of the victim by the morning. His personal life, working life, any form, everything you can find. Any enemies, all his friends, if any. You name it I want it. The press are having a field day with this one and I want it cleaned up as quickly as possible. If this is some kind of ritual killing I want to know who the fuck uses knives like that and who can throw them across a room if necessary with that kind of force and accuracy. Even if you are up all night I want the lot by the morning. This one isn't going to solve itself."

As the door of the lift opened on the ground floor Jimmy's eyes fell on the unmistakable figure of George Milne – the Cat Detective, dressed in what looked like a faded clown's outfit and carrying a bundle of knives identical to the murder weapon. His mouth fell open but he was, for once, speechless, as was DS Young.

George wasn't often quick off the mark but he immediately recognised Jimmy from their dealings on the Frankie Cook case. Perhaps this previous acquaintance could help get George out of the hotel a bit faster than looked likely up till then.

"Hello Sergeant Bell, how are you?" he asked with his best attempt at a friendly greeting.

"What are you doing?" asked Jimmy, finally able to talk.

"I gave up the Cat Detective game. I'm in the knife-throwing business now." George laughed but nobody joined him. "In fact one of my knives is missing, so if you could keep an eye open while you're here in case it turns up I would be grateful."

Lola who was standing behind George looked at the expressions on the faces of the two police officers and suspected they had more important things on their minds.

"It's Inspector Bell now, and I have a few questions I'd like to ask you," said Jimmy, now in full control of his voice again.

....

....

Down at the station George quickly realised that Jimmy was not interested in helping him recover lost property. The rough way that he and Lola were handcuffed and bundled into a police van should have been a warning in itself. At the station he was asked if he wanted to have a solicitor present when he was interviewed. This did get the alarm bells ringing. Reporting lost property didn't usually require a solicitor's presence.

Jimmy came into the interview room with the younger, female officer who had been in the lift with him earlier. A microphone on the table was switched on and Jimmy spoke into it confirming the names of those present, the date and the time. George noticed that Jimmy was still rather angry and suspected some of the rough treatment was due to getting his rank wrong back at the hotel. "Oops," thought George to himself. "Some people are touchy about the smallest things."

"Now George, tell me what you were doing in the Grand Pacific Hotel around ten o'clock yesterday evening."

"Lola had been throwing knives at me for the butlers and afterwards we went for a drink."

It all seemed straight forward to George. Once his pal Jimmy knew the facts George would be off home, with just the little matter of sleeping with Lola to reconcile with Janine.

"Lola?"

"The girl with me at the hotel tonight. She throws knives for a living. She looks like a slip of a girl, even fully dressed, but she can throw those knives hard enough to kill an elephant. Trust me, I've seen her do it first hand."

"You've seen her kill elephants?" asked Jimmy still trying to figure out what the Cat Detective had to do with the murder of Eric Ramsay. He was obviously involved up to his armpits even if it was only as an accomplice to this Lola Cortez aka Theresa Maguire.

"No. I was just saying she could throw them hard enough to kill."

"Who is Eric Ramsay?" Jimmy asked suddenly hoping to catch George out.

George didn't do 'suddenly' and thought for a minute or two.

"Is he the darts player?" he asked in all seriousness.

"If he played darts, he doesn't anymore," Jimmy added. "How do you know him?"

"I don't," replied George quite lost. "I might have seen him on the TV but I'm not too good with names. Is he the fat one or the one with all the jewellery?"

"He was a butler, not a darts player," chipped In DS Young trying to move things forward.

"If he is a butler he might be at the hotel. It's full of butlers at the moment."

"He is at the hotel, he is dead, and he has one of your fucking knives sticking out of his back. Any comments?" Jimmy almost shouted at George, remembering now how obtuse he could be from his previous dealings with him in Coatshill.

"Ah," said George, "Now I understand why you brought me here." George found himself returning automatically to that defensive state he found comforting at such times; a bit slow and perhaps annoying for anyone trying to get straight answers from him. It had worked well whenever he was in trouble at school and he had reverted to it before when questioned by Jimmy Bell or one of his colleagues during the brief excitement in George's life which was Frankie Cook's last few weeks. Jimmy found it infuriating. DS Young just found it confusing.

"Did you know Eric Ramsay?"

"No, not while he was alive."

"Did Lola kill him with one of her knives?"

"No, she only throws them at me."

And so it went on, with the tape running and recording George's every word. The uniformed officer in the corner of the interview room stifled a laugh on more than one occasion. Jimmy stopped himself from common assault at least once. After five minutes DS Young decided they were wasting their time with George and switched off completely. It was far more likely that his girlfriend Lola had done the deed and George was along for the ride, knowingly or unknowingly. If he was guilty of anything he was only guilty of winding her boss up to the point where he would be insufferable for days. She had been delighted to become assistant to a detective with the reputation of Jimmy Bell but this had faded quickly as she decided he may not be the genius she had hoped he was. She felt certain she was learning nothing from him that morning. Jimmy had confided in her before the interview that George had helped with intelligence during the big drugs bust in Lanarkshire which had established his reputation and gained him promotion. As she listened to George answer the questions she wasn't sure the word intelligence could ever be applied to any dealings with him whatsoever.

Chapter Thirty Eight: Jimmy Interviews Lola Cortez aka Theresa Maguire

Jimmy Bell and DS Young eventually gave up interviewing George, much to everyone's relief. The facts established were; George did not appear to know the deceased, he could not throw knives to save himself (or kill someone else for that matter) and he was the most infuriating interviewee in the history of policing. They turned their attentions to Lola Cortez, aka Theresa Maguire, hoping for better luck.

Lola had been brought to the station still wearing her stage costume, much to the amusement of the officers on duty there. She had been held in an interview room with a female officer on guard. Jimmy entered the room expecting to find Lola nervously awaiting his arrival and the uniformed constable standing impassively in the corner. Instead as he opened the door he heard the two finishing a conversation about how useless men could be when drunk.

Jimmy eyed daggers at the young police officer and turned his attention to Lola. As before, he read the date and time into the microphone on the desk along with the names of those present.

"Please confirm your name for the record," he asked Lola in a very business-like manner to try to recreate any nervousness she may previously have felt.

"Lola Cortez, with a Z not an S."

"Please state your full name as it appears on official documents," snapped Jimmy trying to introduce an air of intimidation.

"Which ones?" asked Lola who no longer knew the meaning of intimidated. "My Spanish passport says Lola Cortez, with a Z of course. My British passport says Theresa Margaret Maguire. I have a Colombian driving licence which says I am Lola Theresa Escobar but that is a rather long story; apparently that marriage was never fully ratified although I can assure you it was more than fully consummated."

"Theresa," said Jimmy impatiently, "If I may call you that for simplicity. Tell me about Eric Ramsay."

"Never heard of him," replied Lola in all honesty. "Should I have?"

"I believe so. After all he was found late yesterday evening with one of your knives in his back."

"I had wondered where it had got to, though I had assumed it had simply been stolen."

"We are waiting for confirmation but early indications are that the knife had your fingerprints and George Milne's fingerprints on it but nobody else's. Any comments?"

"It's hardly surprising that it had our fingerprints on it. Whose fingerprints should I be surprised it did not have on it?"

Jimmy was slightly thrown by the question at first but recovered quickly.

"We are at the early stages of this investigation but are not currently interviewing anyone other than yourself and your accomplice, George Milne."

"I prefer to use the term assistant for my act. George simply stands there and looks worried as I throw knives at him; although he is getting rather good at acting out the initial switch. If, however, you are investigating a murder and are not interviewing anyone other than poor George and myself, I imagine the culprit is making a comfortable getaway. "

Jimmy was disappointed to note that Lola did not appear to be nervous or to be even the least concerned that she had been arrested and was being questioned by Police Scotland in connection with a murder. This aroused his suspicions even more. Only an experienced villain would be able to stay so calm during questioning, he thought.

There had to be something between her and the victim, something in their past, and he was determined to find out what it was.

Lola was just bored. She had been interviewed by police in 14 different countries and interrogated by the CIA, the DEA and the FBI. Nobody who appeared anywhere as Lola Theresa Escobar got in or out of the United States or South America without arousing the interest of one or more law enforcement agencies. Add to that the spite of a jealous congressman's wife from Idaho, whose brother went from Chief of Staff at The White House to head up the CIA and you had a worldwide problem when travelling. In comparison to some of her previous 'interviews without coffee', this was a breeze. The only real problem she had with her current predicament was the dress sense of the two detectives. The inspector wore a suit which had probably not encountered a dry cleaner for weeks if not months, and it was poorly matched with a blue shirt and red tie.

The female detective wore the kind of suit which Lola had only ever worn at the request of men who wanted her to dominate them. On those occasions Lola had ensured that the clothes accentuated her curves. DS Young's suit only accentuated that fact that she was not comfortable wearing suits. Lola was sure she could work wonders with her if they could just spend an afternoon together shopping. On this occasion her mistake was to point it out.

"Just answer the fucking questions," snapped Janice, well aware of her sartorial shortcomings and irate at a circus act giving her advice on how to dress.

"Where were you at ten thirty last night?" snapped Jimmy, desperately trying to re-establish the initiative.

Lola thought for a brief second before replying.

"Jumping on top of George's bones; after all, a cock is a cock."

The two police officers looked at each other as they realised any chance of an open and shut case was disappearing into the long grass.

"Do you spend most evenings with George Milne?" Jimmy continued.

"I'm not that desperate," Lola corrected. "I spent the evening before in much grander company."

"Specifically?" demanded Janice no longer in control of her temper.

"A lady doesn't kiss and tell."

"This is a murder enquiry. We need to establish your whereabouts."

"Was Eric Ramsay murdered on both evenings or just last night?"

"He was murdered last night about ten thirty when your alibi was conveniently your boyfriend. Just answer the questions Theresa," snapped Janice who had taken over the questioning to give Jimmy's blood pressure a chance to drop slightly.

"If he was only murdered last night then you only need to know where I was last night. The previous night is irrelevant to your enquiries. If you insist it is then I'll have to insist on having my lawyer present. Oh, and for the record, George is Janine McGovern's boyfriend, not mine. I only borrowed him for my act. Stage act that is; the other acts were spontaneous and definitely on a strictly temporary basis."

Jimmy nodded to Janice to follow him out of the room and turned to the female police officer as he was leaving.

"Just watch her, please," he snapped. "No swapping fucking recipes this time."

She nodded, red faced, and tried to ignore Lola's attempt at restarting their previous conversation.

Outside the interview room Jimmy turned to Janice.

"Thoughts?"

"I have to admit I don't think either of them is guilty of this one boss. He's too stupid and would have blurted out something incriminating by now. She's too relaxed, if not bored, to be sitting there after murdering someone; at least in the last day or two. Before that I wouldn't rule anything out."

"I agree," said Jimmy. "We'll keep them here for another few hours till they give us formal statements. Get uniform to do that. We'll head back to the hotel and see what the staff and guest statements and IDs have turned up. Chase up everything we know about the late Eric Ramsay."

"Will do. Coffee?"

"In the absence of something stronger, yes. Milk and all the sugar you can get in it."

Chapter Thirty Nine: Jimmy Meets Hamish

Back at the hotel Jimmy was about to head for the manager's office when a uniformed sergeant caught his attention and warned him that one of the guests, a Lord Strathbole, was starting to complain about being held bottled up in the hotel and had mentioned in passing that he had spent the previous evening with Assistant Chief

Constable Cooper, who had been his personal guest at the dinner and floorshow.

Jimmy groaned and sent the sergeant to invite Lord Strathbole to the manager's office where Jimmy would personally interview him and let him head off if he so wished. The last thing Jimmy wanted at that particular moment was a complaint reaching the ears of ACC Cooper.

Lord Strathbole appeared at the manager's office and entered without knocking.

"What a dreadful business, Inspector. Thank you for seeing me so quickly on your return. I have a number of pressing engagements today and would like to push off if I may. The rest of the convention has been cancelled, including tonight's Butlers Ball, unfortunately."

"I won't keep you long, Sir," said jimmy. "I just need to ask a few routine questions. Where were you last night between the hours of eight o'clock and ten thirty?"

"I was watching the circus act at dinner with the butlers; sitting next to Assistant Chief Constable Brian Cooper. Do you know him, Inspector?"

"Only too well," thought Jimmy but restricted his answer to a polite, "Yes, Sir."

Lord Strathbole continued, seeing that the mention of Cooper's name had had the desired effect.

"We left the table shortly after the finale which would have been about ten o'clock and went to the bar with some of the committee for more drinks. I believe we were there till at least midnight. ACC Cooper left around then and I headed to my suite. Was there anything else you wished to ask me, Inspector?"

"Did you know the deceased, Eric Ramsay?" asked Jimmy, going through the motions as quickly as he could.

"No, I'm afraid I did not. Somebody said he worked abroad somewhere and hadn't attended before. Sorry I can't be of any more assistance."

"Thank you, Your Lordship, you are free to leave the hotel if you wish."

"Thank you inspector and good luck!"

Jimmy watched Lord Strathbole leave and turned to the list of guests on the desk in front of him. It was going to be a long day.

Chapter Forty: Lola calls her lawyer

The novelty of being arrested in Britain for the first time soon wore off on Lola. Whenever she had been arrested in North or South America she had been acutely aware that she would have to rely on her own devices to get free. In Britain, however, she knew that she had certain rights and decided to put them to good use. After failing to re-engage the female PC in further conversation she instead started to demand her right to a phone call. The details of exactly what she was and was not entitled to were unclear but she was sure she was due at least one phone call.

"I demand to be charged with a crime, released or to be allowed to phone my lawyer," she began.

Turning down the suggestion of waiting until Inspector Bell returned she loudly noted the officer's service number from her lapels and started to threaten her personally with legal action for holding her against her will.

The female officer let the comments bounce off at first, but did start to wonder if her superior could in fact detain someone without charging them or allowing them to speak to a legal advisor for as long as Lola had been there. Eventually she reluctantly agreed to check with her boss to see if a phone call was permissible.

Lola thanked her with exaggerated gratitude and then wondered what to do next. She did not have a lawyer in the UK or indeed know any. She would have phoned George and Janine for their advice were it not for the fact that George was locked up next door and Janine was probably currently considering ways of killing her or George or both. The only other person she could count on at the moment for their support and money if necessary was her agent Benny. She knew he was infatuated with her and would do anything he could in order to gain her gratitude.

After a while the female officer returned and advised Lola that Jimmy Bell had agreed that she could make one phone call to her lawyer but that she should not expect to be released for a while.

Lola took the phone she was handed politely and dialled a number.

"Hi Benny, it's Lola. I need a huge favour."

At the other end of the line Benny listened intently as Lola's plight was explained to him in detail. He had imagined her phoning him a thousand times but none of the scenarios measured up to the reality when the call actually came through. He sympathised, agreed where appropriate and promised action when asked. Before the call ended he had foolishly promised to sort everything out for her.

Lola handed the phone back and smiled at her warden.

"Now the sparks will fly," she assured, with a lot more confidence than she actually felt.

In his office Benny replaced the handset on his desk phone carefully and sat back.

"Oh shit!" was all he could manage to say.

Chapter Forty One: A Booking for Strathbole Castle

Lord Strathbole just could not get Lola out of his mind. While he had enjoyed many a night of passion with beautiful women, Lola seemed to have left him needing to see her again, like an addiction. He was unable to track her down in the hotel after The Butler's Convention for obvious reasons. One of the staff had even suggested Lola had been arrested for the murder of Eric Ramsay. Reports in the newspaper confirmed the police had released their two early suspects and had made no further arrests since. That meant Hamish had to track her down and come up with a suitable excuse to see her again. After a few phone calls to the hotel manager he obtained the contact details of Lola's agent, one Benny Goldflab of London. Further consideration brought inspiration and he realised an upcoming charity event at the Castle would provide a pretext to meet her again.

Lord Strathbole had then called a rather surprised Benny to book a variety act for the 'Ponies in Difficulties' fund raiser.

"I want something a bit different and heard you had a knife-throwing act on your books."

"I got a few, but if you want something unique then go for Lola Cortez. She has a knock-out act, is a real looker and always gets some laughs with her partner; he's a real figure of fun. She can dance too; a really beautiful mover."

"Don't I just know it," Hamish thought to himself.

"I'll need a clown for the children too. Do you have someone in the Perth area?"

Benny wasn't entirely sure what constituted "the Perth Area", or indeed exactly where Perth was, but he was astute enough to agree first and worry about such details later. Lean times were never far away and a booking was a booking. Getting into Lola's good books once more was a huge bonus too although he had been a little disappointed at her lack of gratitude after he spent a lot of time and money arranging her release from recent police custody .

"I know just the clown you need," he lied convincingly.

"Excellent," said Hamish. "Can you arrange for the acts to arrive the day before the event so I can brief them, please? I'll provide a bed for the night at no charge."

"Sure, Mr... Eh Lord Strath..."

"Bole!"

"Of course, your lordship. That will count as a two-day booking though."

"Whatever. I hope I get my money's worth. Phone my factor on this number to confirm the booking as soon as you can."

Chapter Forty Two: Ruth Swanson Reports

Jimmy received a call from Ruth Swanson to say that the post mortem report and her own report were ready and copies were available for him to collect when he was ready.

"Just give me the basics, Ruth," he pleaded.

"In short and off the record, a person considerably shorter than the victim walked up behind him and pushed the knife into his back. It wasn't thrown, if that helps. Want the good news?" she asked and without waiting for a response added, "There were traces of somebody else's blood on the blade near the base. Most likely the murderer's."

"Bingo," said Jimmy.

"The bad news is that it doesn't match either of your friends in the knife-throwing act."

"You're kidding," said Jimmy. "It's got to be that Lola creature."

"No chance. Not even the same type, never mind a DNA match. Your pal George Milne is out of the equation too.

Nor does the DNA match any of the staff or guests at the hotel tested during your interviews. Have a nice day."

The phone went dead and Jimmy sat in his seat rather lost. He had been sure Lola was guilty and George had something to do with it, either consciously, or, more likely in his case, unconsciously.

"Bugger," he said out loud before dialling Janice's extension and telling her to come to his office for an update.

Chapter Forty Three: Making a Clown of George

Lola was delighted to get yet another phone call from Benny with a booking but alarm bells rang when she discovered it was for Hamish Strathbole at his castle. She immediately pictured dungeons and servants in medieval dress, neither of which fazed her, but her night of passion with his lordship was supposed to have been a one-off. She could live without the attentions of an aristocratic stalker. She was though, if nothing else, a very practical girl; being no longer young she needed the work, and so she agreed.

Benny then asked if she knew a clown in the Perthshire area who could entertain the children at the same function. After her time with the circus she had made a point of avoiding clowns and had to answer honestly that she did not. Benny was insistent that the booking was for her and George doing the knife-throwing act and a clown who could keep the children amused throughout the day.

"I don't have anyone on my books in that area and my other clowns are booked that day or won't travel that far north."

"Good grief, Benny, all you need is someone in a clown costume who can fall over things and make kids laugh. Even you could do it."

Benny thought back to his attempts at making people laugh with stand-up and wasn't so sure. He was, however, very keen on the idea of attending the function with Lola, especially as the booking included at least one night at the venue. It might be just the opportunity he had been waiting for to get to know Lola more intimately, although having seen her wiggle in and out of costumes in his office he felt he was already almost there.

"What about George?" asked Lola. "I'm sure he could be a clown after I've thrown my knives at him. I laugh at him all the time and he always falls over things after spinning on the wheel."

"No can do, I'm afraid. The clown act has to entertain the younger children while you're doing your act so it must be somebody different."

"Well it's easy then. George can be the clown and I'll throw my knives at you. I assume you can pop up for the sake of a good customer. I'll talk you through what's required. Just look serious and don't eat too much before the finale."

Benny had already cleared the dates in his diary just in case, but he had had no intention of being the target for Lola's knives. George being a clown was an obvious solution as people were always laughing at him for one reason or another, but the knives were a different matter.

Lola could sense that Benny was wavering at the other end of the phone and didn't want to lose what could turn out to be a bumper pay day.

"Of course it would mean we would have to share a dressing room but you have seen me change before."

"I'll do it," said Benny before he could stop himself.

"Great. I'll sort out George and teach him some basic tricks to amuse the kiddies. See you on the 19th at Strathbole Castle." With that Lola put the phone down.

"Brilliant," said Benny out loud. He was booked to spend the weekend with Lola although it was hardly the romantic trip he had fantasised about.

Chapter Forty Four: George the Clown

It could have been said unkindly that visually, George had been born to be a clown. Not a happy clown of course. No big red smile on George's face. Instead he would be the one constantly saddened by being the butt of the other clowns' practical jokes. He had a naturally sad look on his face and this had been greatly increased by his recent split from Janine. He was not very tall for his weight and had a slumped air in his bearing that suggested life had weighed heavily on his shoulders for some time. The more Lola thought about it the more she thought that George could be, not only a good clown, but perhaps a great clown. She had known some clowns in her time and slept with at least one, so she knew what she was talking about.

All that George needed was the right costume and a little bit of instruction from her. If she could get him to see how naturally funny people found him and get him to play to that strength he could be a star. Benny might even put him on his books. The starting point had to be a bit of intensive instruction and with that in mind she invited him round to the flat in Woodend Walk where she had moved temporarily after the unfortunate confrontation with Janine. Rosie and Carol had headed off for a few days to a festival in the South of England, leaving Evelyn in Lola's dubious care.

George had been reluctant to go at first, blaming Lola for his loss of Janine and keen to end his brief foray into show business, but Lola had been insistent. George's resolve had not been strong enough to resist and so he found himself walking towards 10 Woodend Walk with a swirl of memories clouding his head. Thoughts of Frankie Cook's demise, a close shave with his killers and even poor Miss Blackery, Frankie's next door neighbour, all returned whenever he visited the flat (which had been as rarely as possible).

He arrived at the door and rang the bell. Gone was the steel door with massive bolts which had guarded the premises during Frankie's time there. This had been replaced by a half etched glass/ half oak door of which Miss Blackery would have approved. A voice inside shouted "enter," and he pushed the unlocked door and went inside. Walking through to the living room he found Lola sitting on the sofa leafing through a catalogue of stage costumes, without a stitch of clothing on.

"I've returned to my old habits here. I hope you don't mind?"

George didn't really but was annoyed at Lola sufficiently to briefly suggest that she should put something on for their meeting. He didn't labour the point though when she completely ignored him.

"I know you are angry with me, George, and I completely understand. I seem to have put my foot in it with poor Janine and she has left you, though I suspect it is a temporary huff on her part."

George wasn't so sure but said nothing. Instead he sat down on the chair opposite and simply stared at Lola, even occasionally at her face.

"Truth is, I have decided to tour Europe with my act if possible, obviously with a new partner, but I need you just one more time for a booking I have in Perthshire in a fortnight's time."

George was just about to point out that he had made it quite clear that he would never again be the target of her knife-throwing act under any circumstances when Lola beat him to it.

"I know you will never again be the target of my knife-throwing act, and I respect that; however this is something quite different. My manager Benny has agreed to take over your role for this booking which is actually a charity function at Lord Strathbole's castle. The truth is I have to spend the night there and need someone with me I can trust. I know his Lordship only too well and I suspect Benny has an ulterior motive for agreeing to help me."

George was wrong-footed by Lola's plea for help but not quite convinced.

"There would be no reason for me to be there if Benny is happy to be in the act. If I just tagged along people might be unhappy. Benny for one wouldn't agree, and Lord Strathbole wouldn't pay for me being there or put me up at his expense."

"I've thought of that, dear George, and I've come up with the perfect cover story. The event is a pony-jumping fund raiser and there will be loads of children of all ages. I have arranged for you to be there to protect me in the guise of a clown to entertain the younger kids. Everyone has fallen for it and agreed. You'll even get paid a fee."

George was thrown again. Lola had thought of everything and he was slightly flattered that she wanted him there to ward off the unwelcome advances of Benny and or Lord Strathbole.

"Well…"

Before he could say anything for or against the trip, Evelyn walked into the room without a stitch on.

"Lola says we should be proud of our bodies and not hide them away," she said.

George almost choked at the sight and the inner confusion over a still attractive Evelyn appearing naked, and his duty by default to look after her now her brother was dead.

"I think you should wear something whenever you have a visitor," he eventually managed to say. "What if you had to answer the door to the postman, for example?"

"Oh, he didn't mind," replied Evelyn.

"Still, best pop on a dressing gown or something for the moment."

Evelyn was used to George giving her advice and trusted him now, so she disappeared to her room and returned shortly afterwards wearing a long white dressing gown.

"That's better," he reassured her, having eyed daggers at Lola while Evelyn went to change.

"You really don't know how to relax and enjoy life for what it is," complained Lola with a giggle in her voice before turning to Evelyn. "George is going to come with me to my next booking as a clown to make sure I'm safe."

George was sure he hadn't agreed to any such thing but with Janine most definitely out of his life for now and the prospect of being useful to a beautiful woman who had difficulty keeping her clothes on in his company, he could think of no good reason not to go. So he simply smiled and nodded to Evelyn who smiled back and clapped her hands gently at the prospect. She had always loved clowns and now George was going to be one too. Life was good.

Chapter Forty Five: A Horse Kicks Out

Lord Strathbole was walking across the courtyard of his stables with a troubled mind. He had the charity event the following afternoon of course, but his factor always organised such things with his usual military precision. All Hamish had to do was show up, say a few words and hand over rosettes to gushing kids who loved horses more than people, certainly more than their parents in most cases. That bit of the day was easy enough. His cares were all centred around the recent demise of Eric Ramsay, an event he had looked forward to in advance but which now rather haunted his every waking hour. Guilt would have been too strong a word to use to describe the way he felt. No, it was more a feeling of concern for the future. Billy Winkman had excelled himself this time and it appeared no blame could be levelled at anyone who was actually involved in the conspiracy. The police had no idea Billy had been there, and sitting beside an Assistant Chief Constable for the evening gave Hamish the perfect alibi. Despite all this and a feeling that things had gone better than he could have imagined, he still felt a pang of something when Billy winked a knowing wink at him whenever they met. It was not entirely surprising that he did but Hamish would have preferred it if he didn't. It reminded him each time that his future freedom was now dependent on, not only a member of the working classes, but one with a criminal record for violence who enjoyed the occasional lost evening with a bottle of whisky. On balance he was uncomfortable with that state of affairs but was not sure exactly what to do about it.

As he neared the archway out of the courtyard, Billy Winkman came round the corner leading one of Lord Strathbole's favourite hunters. The massive chestnut stallion called Monty was clearly limping badly and the concern of both men quickly focussed jointly on the animal's suffering.

"What's the problem?" Lord Strathbole asked with the genuine concern he reserved largely for his horses and dogs.

"He must have thrown a shoe and one of the stable hands took him out for a gallop without noticing, stupid bastard. He was limping badly before he realised the problem. Rest assured the lad's limping badly now too, but I'm going to have a good look at Monty's hoof once I've brushed him down. He's jumpy and I don't blame him."

"I'll come with you," said Lord Strathbole, pleased that the guilty stable lad was also now suffering.

It was well into the evening and the light was fading fast, but the stables had a good lighting system and both men knew there would be enough light to examine the horse's hooves. It would take one of them calming the horse at the front end before it would let anyone look at its painful rear leg but both of them had worked with horses most of their lives and adopted the necessary positions to assess the level of damage. This they did once Billy had brushed Monty down and calmed him with his usual natural expertise.

The missing shoe had been obvious when they arrived at Monty's stall, a fact which had Billy again cursing the negligent stable boy. He looked at the shoe and propped it against the side of the stall and handed his riding crop to Hamish before slowly making his way to the rear of the horse and gently rubbing its hindquarters. He looked round at his employer who had taken a firm grasp of the bridle and was also gently soothing his end of the huge beast. Billy judged the moment to be right and moved his hand slowly down the horse's leg a few times before bending down and slowly and carefully lifting up the damaged hoof.

At the horse's head Hamish whispered gently to reassure Monty that he was in good hands, and they were determined to ease his pain. Confident that the horse was now relaxed, he then looked back to see how Billy was getting on with the examination, when he had a sudden thought. Looking from the front past the horse's left ear, through the hoof to Billy's head, he saw a perfect line like the sights of his hunting rifle. It was an opportunity which wouldn't come again, he thought. He quickly swung the riding crop down and whipped it into the stallion's belly with a vicious blow which also caught its sheath. The reaction was immediate. The horse suddenly objected to the humans at both ends, rearing its head violently whilst simultaneously lashing out with its legs at the bent over figure of Billy at its rear. Lord Strathbole's aim was as good as ever and one of the horse's hooves caught Billy a massive blow to the side of his head. Despite his ability to soak up punches in the boxing ring, Billy dropped straight to the ground, out for the count. Hamish, improvising furiously now picked up the horse shoe and keeping a watchful eye on the raging horse, struck Billy two more ferocious blows to the head before checking the now traumatised horse was secured to its stall and slipping out of the stables.

Fortunately there was nobody about by that time and Lord Strathbole made it back towards the castle unseen. As he passed the walled garden he realised he still had the horseshoe in his hand. He looked inside the garden to make sure there was nobody around and threw the horseshoe under a thick bush. He resolved to move it again in the morning at a suitable time when horseshoes were being thrown as routinely as toys from the cots of the teenage competitors the following day. One more wouldn't be noticed in the paddock and the farrier who was coming along to provide cover for any eventuality would no doubt collect it up with the others for re-use.

He let himself in via the small door near to the gardens using a key which only he held and changed in time for pre-dinner drinks: his first of the day and, he noted unusually, also the first for his wife that day. They had friends staying that night in preparation for the fund-raiser the next afternoon and Fiona had shown superhuman effort by drinking tea with them in the afternoon and waiting until six to have an alcoholic drink of any kind.

The evening was a delightful one with everyone laughing and joking about horses, dogs and children without a care in the world. Even Hamish felt that way. He was sure Billy was dead when he left him but if not, a night in the cold stables would surely finish him off. It was as if a weight had been lifted from his shoulders and the ninth Lord Strathbole was able to relax and enjoy the company of friends for the first time in a while. Admittedly he had a day of screaming children to endure the next day but that was all part of being who he was. He even found himself staring at his wife in a way he hadn't done for years. Sober and properly dressed up she was still rather tasty, he thought to himself.

Chapter Forty Six: George the Clown at the Castle

Before the event everyone concerned had thought George would make an ideal clown. The proof, however, was in the reaction of the children on the day. After sandwiches, ice cream and far too many sugary drinks, a group of some forty children sat in the walled garden of Strathbole Castle eagerly awaiting the arrival of Fat Geordie the Clown. George had been unaware of his billing until the last moment and had been unimpressed at Benny's choice of name. Lola had assured him it was based on the padding he was wearing and that there were very few clown names which had not already been taken.

He therefore found himself dressed and about to be introduced to the children as Fat Geordie the clumsiest clown in the world. Lola had covered the basics and assured him that young children would laugh at anything a clown did as long as he kept falling over. He remained unconvinced but it was too late now. Lola needed him here to protect her and the only way had been to bring him along as the children's entertainer.

As he heard one of the adults finish their introduction, which had wound the children up to fever pitch he shuffled forward in his outsized shoes, ready to go through the routine he had practised under Lola's guidance.

The shoes were indeed huge and stuck out slightly to the side. As a result they were always catching on things, and today was no exception. As he moved towards the marker he had placed in front of the area where the children were sitting, his right shoe snagged on a bramble vine growing unnoticed under one of the hedges. George rounded the end of the hedge unaware that he was caught up in the thorns of the weed. He made his way towards the marker but well short of it the thorny branch went tight, toppled his already shaky balance and he fell head first onto the grass in front of the children. They went wild, cheering and laughing.

George was panicking. His right shoe was still held fast by the bramble thorns and he was six feet away from the place to start his act. He turned round to free it, still on the ground and got one of his gloves caught in the thorns too. He tried to get back on his feet but tumbled again before he got upright. The children howled with laughter.

George was furious with the bramble bush and managed to plant both feet firmly on the ground, bending his shoes in the process. With a huge effort he pulled on his captor until the vine snapped and he shot forward, doing an awkward forward roll, and ending up almost exactly on his marker, leaving one glove still attached to a thorn in the process. He could start his act now and maybe nobody would notice. He looked up at the children, ready to say hello in the silly voice he had been practising to find that they were already in fits of laughter. Not sure why, George began to go through the routine he had prepared. Unfortunately the first part involved removing his gloves in an exaggerated manner. As he raised his hands to start, he realised one of them was missing. Turning round he saw it stuck on a thorn.

Maybe the kids wouldn't notice too much if he quickly retrieved it and started the act again. He turned to look at the children and they were laughing and shouting away. Good, he thought, they are happy about something. He walked over to the glove and, picking up the bramble vine with his gloved hand, gently peeled the missing glove with his bare hand. It came lose, but as he tried to drop the weed he realised the other glove was now caught. He tried to pull it off with a mighty tug but instead the glove flew off his hand.

"Bugger it," he thought to himself, "I'll just do it with one glove."

He returned to the marker ready to start the act and found the children laughing so much that some of them looked as if they might be sick. He was annoyed. It's not funny, he thought to himself. You try doing this in these stupid shoes.

He started pulling off the remaining glove as he had practised hoping for a big laugh at the end as he tried to pull his fingers off too but the kids couldn't wait. They were now laughing at his every move; even if he didn't move. He was bemused; a fact accentuated by the downturned expression Lola had painted around his mouth. He muddled his way through the rest of his act, falling over on cue, which made his bow-tie spin each time and found the children laughing uncontrollably throughout. At the end he took a bow and his audience, including the adults supervising the children, clapped enthusiastically.

He made his way around the hedge and out of sight, getting caught again on the brambles and falling on the way. As he re-joined Lola and Benny behind the hedge he could hear a chant of "Geordie, Geordie" ringing out behind him.

"You were magnificent, George," said Lola kissing him on the cheek.

"You're a natural, my boy. I loved the way you improvised there," Benny added, shaking George's hand vigorously. "It takes real talent to do that. I never got laughs like that when I was doing stand-up."

George and Lola laughed, then realised Benny wasn't laughing.

"No, it's not a joke. I never got laughs like that from an audience. What's funny?"

As they were about to head off to the tent containing food and drink, Simon Peter Strathbole appeared beaming from ear to ear. He introduced himself and started raving about the act while simultaneously admiring Lola.

"That was magnificent. Some years the children's entertainer has been a bit of a let-down and if the children aren't happy they have a way of spoiling the whole day for everyone. I'll give you a shout when we need the next performance," and with that he shook George and Benny's hands and headed off.

"I need to do that again?" asked George.

"Yes. You're booked for three sets today, 2, 3 and 4 o'clock. Piece of cake really. Talking of cake, I'm off to the food tent."

George was not impressed. So much so that he decided against reminding Benny not to eat too much before the finale of the knife-throwing act. Although it had gone down well with his target audience, George was not sure he could repeat the success of his first clown act again, never mind another twice. He resolved that if he did need to repeat the act it would be without the intervention of the bramble vine which had hampered his earlier entrance. Borrowing Lola's Leatherman multi-tool which she never seemed to travel without, he dived into the hedge to do battle with the brambles.

As he got within cutting distance of the main root he noticed a horseshoe sitting amongst the roots of the hedge. Although he wasn't in the least bit superstitious, he felt a sudden need for all the luck he could get, and so he carefully picked it up and placed it inside the kit bag he had brought to hold his props and change of clothes, taking the precaution to place it inside the empty sandwich bag in case there was any trace of horse germs attached to it. Then he set about the bramble's root, ensuring that it would not interfere with his next performance.

When he went through the act again, without the brambles catching on to his shoes, George was a shadow of his earlier self as a clown and although he felt it went better, the laughs from his young audience were quieter and less enthusiastic. There was polite applause from the adults present but he could tell they were unimpressed and he headed back round the bush on a bit of a low. Lola and Benny were off doing the knife-throwing act for the parents and older children, and he could tell from the noise of their audience that Benny had found his calling as a straight man. He expected to find their little camp of bags and props to be deserted but instead he found Lord Strathbole rooting about the hedge where the offensive bramble bush had been growing until recently.

"Don't worry; I got rid of it, your Lordship," he said as he sat down beside his bag.

"What?" said Lord Strathbole, suddenly in a panic.

"The bramble bush," said George, completely confusing his host. "I'm surprised your gardener didn't spot that one. Nearly ruined my act the first time round but I've cut it back to the roots and dumped the bits on your compost heap. No extra charge."

Hamish looked at the clown sitting in his walled garden and thought there was something familiar about him but couldn't quite place it.

"Oh... thanks," he mumbled absent–mindedly and wandered off, having decided to retrieve the horseshoe and dispose of it later when everyone had gone home.

"Seems keen on his garden," thought George to himself, as he took off his clown's shoes and rubbed his aching feet. He had decided that if nobody could find him he could not be forced to complete the final performance of the day. He didn't need the money and had only agreed to the gig after Lola pleaded with him. As things turned out it looked like Benny was the next one in her sights, and in some ways that suited him just fine. If they headed off round Europe or the world together he would be able to return to a quiet life. At this exact point in time that prospect rather appealed to him. He swapped the clown's shoes for his own loafers, walked over to his car to dump his kit bag and headed for the house to find a good place to hide until the excitement had all died down. In a castle this size there must be somewhere he could hang out. Somewhere that Lola, Benny, the factor and even Lord Strathbole himself couldn't find him till it was too late to be a clown. The kitchen door was open and inviting and it looked as if there were a whole host of rooms above it promising sanctuary.

Chapter Forty Seven: George meets Nanny MacPhee

George sought refuge in the rooms behind the large kitchen, slipping through as inconspicuously as someone in a clown's costume could. The connecting door gave access to a long corridor with a staircase at both ends. Economy wallpaper and faded paint suggested that this was the servant's quarters. Keen to get as far away as possible from the scene outside, George quickly climbed the first staircase and found himself facing a corridor almost identical to the one downstairs, with doors off both sides. He heard a raised voice below him and darted into the first doorway to his left which was slightly ajar. The room beyond was in darkness and he initially thought it unoccupied as a result. After a second or two though, he heard a frail voice call out, "Is that you Annie?"

As his eyes accustomed to the darkness he managed to make out the figure of an old lady sitting in a wing chair beside a bed. She called out again and George felt obliged to respond in case she alerted the household to his whereabouts.

"It's not Annie," he said, "it's George."

"George?"

"George Milne; the clown."

"What clown? The only clown I remember here worked at the Home Farm." With that, the old lady chuckled to herself.

George relaxed. "I'm the children's entertainer. I thought I could maybe change in here but didn't realise there was someone about. Sorry."

"Change here if you like, young man. I'm as blind as a ninety year old bat, so it won't make any difference to me if you do. Anyway, I was the nanny here for years and have seen everything there is to see in my time, before, during and after getting married."

George could see reasonably well in the gloom now and took in his surroundings as the old lady spoke. The bedroom was furnished with essentials as you might expect but the most obvious feature was the vast array of ornaments and mementos on every shelf and flat surface. There were jugs and small flower vases with the names of almost every European capital. Along one wall were hung six large, wooden units stuffed with thimbles; again although he couldn't make them out he could tell they were the kind of reminders people brought back from holiday. On a dressing table he could see a collection of photographs, but again couldn't make out the details.

The old lady had continued to talk of her time as nanny to the Strathboles and seemed to be indicating one of the photographs.

"Put the light on, deary, and you'll see it on the dressing table."

George had made out the name Churchill and out of curiosity put the main light on and walked over to the photographs. Sure enough there was a picture of the extended Strathbole family sitting in front of the house with Winston Churchill in the middle of the group. To the rear, a far younger version of the nanny was dutifully displaying a very young infant to complete the range of generations present at the time.

"That's quite a claim to fame," George enthused, genuinely impressed. "You must have a lot of happy memories?"

"Many. Of course, that photograph was taken just after the war when Winston hadn't been re-elected; such a shame. He seemed to be at a bit of a loose end without the Germans to fight and came here to paint and write. He and Hamish's father had served together in the first world war when Churchill joined a Scottish regiment so he could get a drink."

George had forgotten the guests and children downstairs by now and was listening to the old lady with interest. Partly she reminded him of his gran who had told him stories of the wars but also she seemed pleased to have company of any kind, even his, which made him feel useful.

As she talked he gazed at the pictures of the nanny with a young man in uniform, assorted Strathboles and staff outside the house and a few of people in faraway exotic places. There was also a group of photographs of babies, each one containing a wispy lock of hair. Two pictures which sat side by side caught his eye. One had Lord Strathbole and young Simon Peter in front of the house giving Nanny an enormous bouquet of flowers and an outsized '90 years today' birthday card. The neighbouring one appeared to have a far younger nanny standing beside the staff at the kitchen door, accompanied by a grown up Simon. The age gap of the nanny suggested some 30 or forty years, but the young man was around the age of young Strathbole today.

"That's a clever photo of you in the walled garden with the staff and young Simon. Photo-shopped?" asked George.

"No, the photographer's shop was long closed by then. The factor took that one."

"But Simon looks the same age as he is today?" enquired George more than a little confused. The figure in the picture was the spitting image of Simon Peter down to the unmistakable dark eyebrows contrasting with the luxuriant mop of hair.

"I don't understand," said the nanny. "That photo is of the staff in the walled garden. It was taken before Simon was born."

"But the figure standing to your right; who's that?"

"That's that rascal Eric Ramsay. I imagine he came to no good!"

"Eric Ramsay?" repeated George for confirmation.

"Yes. He would chase anything in a skirt. In the end he was packed off to Europe, never to be heard of again."

George stared again at the two pictures. It could have been the same person, right enough, if they hadn't been taken thirty or forty years apart.

"Well I never," he said, pocketing the framed photograph of Simon Peter Strathbole as a baby, which also contained a lock of his hair.

Chapter Forty Eight: The Bad Penny

Jimmy Webb arrived at Strathbole Castle with a sense that he was on a fool's errand. The death of a stable hand was a serious matter, he had to admit, but in the absence of any proof to the contrary it appeared to be a tragic accident. The Health and Safety Executive may have a legitimate interest in the event, but otherwise it was hardly a matter for a senior CID officer; especially one with a definite murder to solve elsewhere.

He drove up the long driveway, failing to admire the rhododendrons or the vast selection of non-native trees. Even the castle itself did not impress him, no doubt to the disappointment of its long dead architect. The row of expensive cars parked at the front of the house hardly registered in his consciousness. He knew there was a function on and had expected as much. No, he just didn't want to be there. He had Eric Ramsay's killer to hunt down and the only reason he was here was because his superior officer had sent him, to impress all those present that Police Scotland were taking the Strathboles' loss seriously. Jimmy had been tempted to argue back but the distant connection between his current case and Lord Strathbole had made him vaguely curious so he had kept quiet and done what he was told.

On the driveway at the front of the house was a small sign which indicated the stables were off to the rear left of the castle, and Jimmy drove past the line of cars in the direction indicated. He rounded a large clump of bushes and could see the local patrol car still in attendance. It had been parked out of sight of the castle and formal gardens and the officers were nowhere to be seen, discretion being the order of the day. Jimmy found them inside the stable block with cups of tea and plates of cakes and sandwiches nearby. When he walked through the doorway the officers struggled quickly to their feet, easier for the young constable than the ageing and overweight sergeant.

Jimmy nodded at them both then asked the sergeant, "What have we got then?"

"Looks like a temperamental horse kicked a stable hand to death. The factor found him this morning when he came to get his own horse for a morning ride, called an ambulance, and he was pronounced dead at the scene. Open and shut one by the look of it, Sir. The deceased was one William Winkman aged 48. He'd worked here for about ten years. Staff say he had a gift with horses."

"Not this one," Jimmy chipped in. "Go on."

"Kept himself to himself even on race days. The only other thing is he had form. Thumped a couple of police while under the influence being the highlight; did six years, mainly in Perth for that one. Clean since as far as we know. Seems Lord Strathbole took him under his wing and turned his life around. Nothing to add to that really."

Jimmy nodded again. "Have you interviewed his lordship yet?"

"No not yet. Maid said he'd pop down later." The sergeant paused before adding, "I was going to but… eh….The Assistant Chief Constable's here with his wife and kids for the fund raiser and he suggested we made ourselves scarce till later, what with it being an accident and all that."

"You're joking? Which Assistant Chief? Cooper?"

"Cooper."

"Shit!"

"Yes Sir, Shit!"

ACC Cooper was ruthlessly ambitious almost to the point of criminality and had more society connections than BT. If he was here socially then any unpleasantness could be career-threatening for any other policeman involved. Jimmy knew that low profile would be required and that he had been summonsed as mere window dressing for a smooth operation to deal with the selfish bastard who had chosen to get kicked to death by a horse during an

important social event attended by the assistant chief
constable and his pony-obsessed wife and daughter. In
normal circumstances Jimmy might have made a point of
seeking out Lord Strathbole and interviewing him, but
Cooper wasn't normal in any circumstances so he
decided instead to help himself to a cake and wait.

As he ate the rather tasty Paris Brest he had a wander
around the scene of Billy Winkman's demise. The stall
where he had been kicked was taped off and the horse
had long since been removed by the factor to allow for
the removal of Billy's body. The guilty party was feeding
in the neighbouring stable largely untroubled by its recent
actions. It was a large and powerful looking brown hunter
with a white patch on its nose. Jimmy had to admit he
wouldn't like it to kick him anywhere, never mind three
times in the head. Billy had obviously been unluckily in
the wrong place at the wrong time.

After what seemed a very long time Lord Strathbole
entered the stables. He did not seem in the least surprised
to see Jimmy Bell and casually joked, "We must stop
meeting like this."

Sensing that the police were less than amused when
dealing with a violent death he immediately changed
tack. "Dreadful business this. He was a good worker and
normally so good with the beasts. Just goes to show you
can never fully trust one."

"Thanks for sparing your time, your Lordship, I appreciate you are busy. I just need to confirm a few points, then I can finish things here."

"Only too happy to help. Your Assistant Chief Constable was just speaking very highly of you. Anything I can do to assist the police."

"How long had Mr Winkman worked for you?"

"Ten, maybe fifteen years. As I say, he was usually great handling horses. I gave him a job when he was rather down on his luck."

"When he came out of prison?"

"Indeed," said Lord Strathbole. "I see you have done your homework, inspector. Yes, I saw him at a race meeting and remembered him riding some impressive winners before his brush with the law. I felt sorry for him and needed someone here who could work with horses, especially the bigger, more spirited ones I use for hunting. Until today he was never any bother at all."

"I'm sure he regrets being a bother to you today more than anyone," Jimmy added before he could stop himself.

"I didn't really mean a bother, Inspector. An unfortunate turn of phrase perhaps," but it was clear Lord Strathbole resented the implication.

"I'll need to have a word with the person who found him - your factor, I believe?"

"Yes. Capt Gregory, James. He served with me in the same cavalry regiment. He found poor Billy when he came to get a horse for his morning ride. If you pop round to the kitchen when you're finished here I'll have James meet you there. He's judging the pony-jumping at the moment so I'm sure he'll be glad of a break. Was there anything else, Inspector?"

"Not for the moment, thank you, Your Lordship, you have been most helpful."

"For the moment? Surely this was an obvious accident. I don't expect to go over this again."

"I'm sure that won't be necessary, but it will be for the fiscal to decide if an inquiry is needed."

"Oh, of course," Lord Strathbole nodded as if he had assumed Jimmy would be making the final decision there and then. With that he headed back to his guests.

"An old friend, Sir?" enquired the sergeant sensing an undercurrent of dislike between the two men.

"Hardly that, but our paths have crossed before. Always seems to be a body involved. Maybe he spreads bad luck as he goes. Anyway, you two stay here and I'll interview the galloping Captain Gregory. With a bit of luck we can all piss off after that and do something useful."

Jimmy wasn't quite sure where the kitchen was but assumed it would be round the back of the castle somewhere. He walked slowly round the building via the side of the walled garden, wondering all the way what it must be like to be born into all this, and why ACC Cooper insisted on brown-nosing with the Strathboles of this world. He was still bloody annoyed at being dragged away from his current case and being trotted out here like some performing animal in a circus. As he rounded the rear corner of the castle he literally bumped into George Milne, dressed as a clown, who was hurrying in the opposite direction."

"Now it really is a circus," he thought to himself.

"What the fuck are you doing here, George?" he asked, unable to hide his surprise and annoyance.

"Inspector Jimmy, am I glad to see you," said George.

"I can tell from the smile on your face," said Jimmy sarcastically. "Now answer the question. What are you doing here when there's another body been found?"

"Not with a knife in it? We've got all of ours; honest."

"No, this one had been kicked to death by a horse. You don't have horses by any chance?"

"No, just the big knives. I'm here because they needed a clown."

"A career you were born to. Is your girlfriend still throwing knives at you?"

"No, she throws them at her manager now," said George, sounding a little disappointed.

"I'll watch out for his body next then," said Jimmy. "Anyway, why are you glad to see me?"

"I know who Eric Ramsay's son is."

"Eric Ramsay didn't have a son. He had two daughters. What have you got to do with Ramsay anyway? You told me you didn't know him."

"I didn't while he was alive, but I've learned a bit about him now he's dead."

"George, make sense within the next five seconds or I will not be held responsible for my actions." Only the mention of Eric Ramsay had prevented Jimmy from brushing George aside and continuing to his pointless interview in the kitchen.

"It was Nanny MacPhee who gave the game away although her name is actually McIntosh not MacPhee. It was a joke."

Jimmy showed no signs of laughing so George continued.

"She was the only one who kept a photo of Eric from when he worked here. All the other staff have left or died, and she's blind, so she doesn't realise."

"George, I don't have time for your shite at the moment. My boss has wasted enough of my valuable time without you doing the same. At least I can punch you, feel better, and nobody will care. So fuck off and let me get on." Jimmy was angry by now and gave George a mighty shove which resulted in him falling backwards onto his bottom, a force which set off his revolving bow-tie.

"Eric must have shagged Lady Strathbole!" he shouted as he hit the ground.

Jimmy had started towards the kitchen but stopped and turned to George, "What are you talking about?"

"Nanny MacPhee has photos of Eric and young Simon Peter Strathbole and they are identical. Their eyebrows don't match !"

Jimmy stared at George as if trying to make sense of a Chinese puzzle. "How can they be identical if their eyebrows don't match?"

"You're not listening. They both have the same eyebrows which don't match their hair. Eric must have been Simon Peter's dad!"

"If I can translate from your haverings...... You're saying the late Eric Ramsay worked here at some point in the dim and distant past, and that he is the real father of Lord Strathbole's son and heir?"

"Yep. I've got a DNA sample here to prove it."

With that George pulled the framed baby photo of young Simon Peter from his pocket with its tuft of hair clearly enclosed within the glass.

"Where did you get that?" asked Jimmy.

"I had to steal it from Nanny MacPhee, but I knew you wouldn't mind."

"You're not saying this photo of Simon looks like Eric at the same age, are you, because if you are I will definitely punch you."

"No, of course not. The two photos are in Nanny MacPhee's room above the kitchen. I saw this and knew the DNA would match Eric's."

"You'd better be right about this, Milne, or I'll jail you for theft of a photo, wasting police time and... and... taking the piss."

"I'll show you," said George and he headed back the way he had come from.

Jimmy wasn't sure what he had just learned, or whether or not it was important, but there was something in the back of his mind telling him that George had helped in the past and, as unlikely as it may seem, just might be on to something again. He followed George as much out of curiosity as conviction.

The two men headed back into the kitchen and Jimmy followed George as he headed to the servants' quarters, hoping that if James Gregory was waiting for him there he wouldn't realise who was following the clown around just yet. At the top of the stairs George indicated the room and went in first.

"Hello again Nanny MacPhee. It's George the clown again. I brought a friend to look at your photographs."

"Is he a clown too?" asked the old lady.

"I hope not," Jimmy whispered under his breath.

George went over to the dresser as the elderly nanny started talking away to her second guest of the day, again delighted at the company but not entirely sure why so many people had chosen to visit her. Maybe it was the charity event downstairs, she decided.

Jimmy followed George to the dresser and looked at the two photos which were handed to him. In the first he saw a group of staff pictured by the walled garden with a younger version of the nanny in the front row. Beside her was a striking young man who looked like a tall version of Robert Redford, complete with a mop of golden hair. Instead of matching golden eyebrows he had a pair which were dark and bushy. The other photo had a now elderly nanny with Lord Strathbole and a young man identical to the one in the other photo. As George had realised, the differing age of the nanny precluded the two being the same person.

"Well I'll be buggered," said Jimmy out loud.

"That's not very nice language for a clown to use in front of an old lady," said the Nanny, chuckling as she said it.

<u>Chapter Forty Nine: Billy Winkman was murdered.</u>

Jimmy sat in his office thinking through the events of the previous day. The more he thought them through, though, the less he seemed to understand them. It had to be more than a coincidence that he had now met Lord Strathbole twice within a matter of weeks and that each time there was a dead body involved, George Milne was there and Lord Strathbole had ACC Cooper as an alibi. He just could not figure out the connection. Lord Strathbole could not have murdered Ramsay, even though he had the motive, as he undoubtedly knew that his ex-butler was the father of Simon Peter Strathbole. His claim that the name Eric Ramsay meant nothing to him was clearly a lie which immediately made him a suspect. He could have arranged for Cooper to be with him on each occasion as the perfect alibi as well as being a person likely to prevent too much scrutiny of his movements if requested to do so. And what about the late unlamented Billy Winkman? Why had a horse decided to kick his groom to death while Cooper was staying at Strathbole Castle? It was unfortunate, or perhaps very fortunate, timing but it certainly looked like the horse was the guilty party there.

The other thing which was annoying Jimmy Bell was the way his assistant appeared to have lost a certain degree of respect for him. Ramsay's death was the first big murder case they had worked on together and until it began she had showed the same respect for her boss that others in the division had done, based on his reputation from the west coast. He was the Detective Sergeant who had put away some of the biggest players in the drugs scene there, making others flee the country or shut up shop. As a result he was assumed to be the man who could make a similar impact in and around Edinburgh when he arrived on promotion to Detective Inspector. Janice had specifically requested the post as his assistant, hoping to learn from the best. The fact that most of his success in Coatshill came from a chance connection with George Milne the so-called cat detective remained his secret. Now he felt he was being judged by his junior colleague and he didn't like it, even if it was based on lack of results to date. What he needed was a breakthrough. He wasn't likely to have similar luck solving this case. That would be far too much to hope for.

The phone rang and when he answered it he heard Ruth Swanson's voice at the other end.

"Busy?" she asked.

"Of course I'm busy; I have a murder to solve," replied Jimmy.

"Well, Jimmy, my old mate, now you have two."

"What do you mean?" asked Jimmy slightly confused.

"My colleague has just been contacted by the medic dealing with Billy Winkman's apparent argument with a horse as it turns out after the horse put the boot in, somebody else hit him hard. Coincidentally, with a horse shoe."

"You're kidding. How do they know?"

"The first kick from Monty the horse was with a hoof which had lost a shoe. The next two were with the edge of a shoe which had a twisted nail in the middle. A shoe which could not have been on the horse's other hoof, going by the angle of impact. I assume you didn't come across a large horseshoe at the crime scene?"

"I didn't even think it was a crime scene at the time," admitted Jimmy starting to seriously worry about his future now. "Are you sure about all of this?"

"Yep. You are about to find out officially from on high, but I thought I'd better warn you. Good luck finding the murder weapon."

"I'll need it," said Jimmy. "A horse trainer's stables with thirty thoroughbreds just after a pony club event with a hundred visiting animals. It will be like looking for the proverbial needle in the hay stack even if it is still anywhere on the premises. Thank you Ruth; you have ruined an already perfectly miserable day."

"I like to spread the love when I can," said Ruth, who then hung up.

Jimmy waited for the inevitable shit to hit his fan as the accidental death of a groom which he had been sent to check out was officially re-categorised as a murder. Soon enough he was summonsed to his boss's office. A bollocking ensued and he was told to sort it out. A call confirming the cause of Billy's death was followed by a report which arrived by email shortly afterwards. As a result of all this activity it was some time before he could sit down and think through the implications of the news. If Billy had been murdered then there was almost certainly a connection between his murder and Eric Ramsay's. It stood to reason that the suspects were likely to be or include those who were present at both venues. That meant Lord Strathbole, ACC Cooper, Theresa Maguire and George fucking Milne. He didn't fancy starting with Lord Strathbole and ACC Cooper was a man to be avoided, even with good news. That left Les Cortez.

He was just about to grab his coat and track down George Milne, hopefully at home, when his phone rang again. Bracing himself for more bad news, he was surprised to hear Ruth's voice again.

"You owe me dinner now," she said.

"How come?" asked Jimmy again confused.

"I have a match for the blood on the knife which killed Eric Ramsay."

"Honestly?"

"Yes, and you're not going to believe whose it is."

"It has to be Milne or Maguire. There had to be a mistake first time around."

"Now you owe me two dinners; the second one as an apology. I don't make mistakes" said Ruth sounding genuinely annoyed.

"Sorry, Ruth, it's been a bad morning and I was hoping for a neat solution. Whose blood was it?"

"Maybe it will prove easy now. The blood on Eric Ramsay's murder weapon was Billy Winkman's. Have fun."

As Jimmy put his phone down he started to take in the implications of this latest revelation. Billy murdered Eric and was then himself murdered, with his death made to look like an accident. Eric was the real father of Lord Strathbole's son and had worked for him, despite the fact that his Lordship had not mentioned that fact at the first interview. Billy was a violent ex-con who also worked for Lord Strathbole and owed him big time for giving him a job after he came out of jail. Everything pointed to Strathbole but he had the world's strongest alibi each time: ACC Cooper, who had testified that he was with his mate Hamish all of the evening that Billy was murdered and definitely at the estimated time of death, which had been between the beef wellington and the soufflé of the dinner party.

Now Jimmy had to set up a full murder enquiry with the inevitable search of Strathbole Castle grounds for the horseshoe and a re-interview with Cooper to confirm the timings of Hamish's alibi.

"Shit," he thought to himself, needing time to think of the best way of approaching all of that. On balance he thought he would go and interview George and Theresa first, if only to delay the unpleasant steps to come. He'd had a shitty morning so far, and worse was to come, so why not go and make somebody else's life a misery for a while, just to feel better. He could think of nobody more deserving of it than that clown George Milne and his knife-throwing pal from Drumchapel. It might be a pointless trip, but he knew he would feel better afterwards and be ready to face whatever lay ahead.

Chapter Fifty : Jimmy Bell's déjà vu

Jimmy walked up the path to George's front door with a sense of déjà vu. He was also curious to see how many zebras there were living in the house these days. He had never managed to get the vision of them out of his mind and could never quite figure out what George got up to with them. He gave the door a proper policeman's knock and stood back.

After a few seconds George answered the door dressed in a wolf-pattern onesie.

"Hello, Mr Bell," said George, playing safe with his rank this time. "Can I help you?"

"I want to ask you a few questions about your recent visit to Strathbole Castle, and possibly some about the Butlers' Ball. Can I come in?"

As Jimmy was talking he noticed Lola Cortez run from the living room to one of the bedrooms completely naked, followed shortly afterwards by a blonde who also wore nothing. Both women were giggling away to themselves.

"How does he do it?" Jimmy thought to himself.

"Of course, come in," said George, who left the door for Jimmy to close and walked through to the living room. Jimmy followed him, half expecting and fully hoping to see more naked women there. He was disappointed that the room was empty and he sat down on the sofa and faced George who had also sat down and was beginning to sip on a fresh cup of coffee. As before, there was no offer of a cup for Jimmy, so he got down to business.

"You will be aware that one of Lord Strathbole's grooms was killed by a horse the day of the charity fund raiser where you appeared as a clown"

Although it was spoken as a question George took it as a statement and remained silent.

"You were aware of that, weren't you?" prompted Jimmy.

"Yes, we had heard from one of the staff."

"Well, to cut a long story short, we are now treating it as murder, and I wondered if you could help me by going through everything that happened from the moment you arrived till the moment you left. I'd like to have a word with Theresa too."

"Who?"

"Lola Cortez. She can put some clothes on first if she prefers."

George was a little shocked. He was starting to think that people were likely to be murdered wherever he went and wondered if he should stay home more often. He began to run through the events of the few days spent at Strathbole castle, with Jimmy stopping him occasionally to clarify points as he went. Jimmy took some notes along the way.

After George had finished, Jimmy showed him a picture of Billy Winkman and asked if he had ever seen him at the castle or at the Grand Pacific Hotel. George took a good look at the picture and shook his head.

"No I've never seen him before at either place. Whoever killed him really made a mess of him, didn't they?" said George trying to be chatty for once.

"The picture's from years ago after a boxing match, although he did look similar when he was found dead. Did anybody mention the name Billy Winkman in your hearing while you were there?"

"No. It's a pretty unusual name, I would have remembered and he is a fairly distinctive looking bloke. Do you think this has anything to do with Eric Ramsay and Lord Strathbole not being his son's father?"

Jimmy looked at George, conscious that he had again provided the best lead in a case and wanting to give him at least some encouragement.

"I don't know for certain, but it is all too much of a coincidence for the two deaths not to be related. Lord Strathbole has alibis for each murder, one of which is a senior police officer who can vouch for him on both occasions."

"Maybe the senior policeman did it. Could he have killed both of them?"

"Only if they stood in the way of him becoming Chief Constable; then he would be our main suspect. No, we can discount him. There has to be a link between the two murders which involves Lord Strathbole, but without a bit of luck I can't seem to prove it."

"You should borrow my horseshoe; maybe it will bring you luck. It hasn't worked for me since I found it."

Jimmy looked at George with a strange expression. "What horseshoe?"

"The one I found in the bushes at Strathbole Castle."

"When did you find it?"

"Between performances."

Jimmy was on his feet and had a hold of George's onesie near the throat.

"Show me," he demanded.

George led the way to his bedroom and took the sandwich bag with the horseshoe in it from its resting place on his bedside table.

"I was going to clean it up but Lola said that would wash all the luck away. What do you think?"

Jimmy looked at the horseshoe with its bent nail sticking out of the central hole and the dried blood around the middle as if he had just found the Holy Grail.

"Oh she is right. You would have washed all the fucking luck out of this horseshoe alright."

Jimmy took another plastic bag from his pocket and placed the sandwich bag and horseshoe inside.

"I'll be back to get a statement from you soon. Don't go anywhere, do you hear me?" he said in such a way that George almost handed him his passport to convince him he wouldn't dream of it.

Jimmy left almost running through and out of the house, so intent on his piece of good luck that he didn't even notice the two zebras walking through to the living room from the kitchen. When he reached his car he immediately dialled a saved number on his phone.

"Ruth? Drop everything you're working on. I've found the needle in the haystack."

<u>Chapter Fifty One: Good Lord ?</u>

Jimmy dropped the horseshoe off at Ruth's lab and looked set to wait for any secrets it might give up as she carried out the tests. Ruth knew what Jimmy was like, and eventually chased him back to his own office to wait for her call. Once there he waited on tenterhooks. Things weren't helped by the presence of Janice his assistant, which racked up the pressure several notches.

"I know you don't want to give away your sources, boss, but just how did you get hold of the horseshoe?"

Jimmy sat back in his chair trying desperately to exude an air of calm professionalism. Thinking through how Sherlock Holmes might have put it, especially played by Basil Rathbone, he put on a rather patronising tone which really pissed off his colleague.

"It seemed clear to me that there had to be a link between Eric Ramsay's murder and the death of Billy Winkman at Strathbole Castle. It was too much of a coincidence not to be, and old Hamish Strathbole had to be involved. If Billy had been bludgeoned to death with a horseshoe, it stands to reason that it would have been left around by the killer rather than risk being caught disposing of it. Where better to hide a horseshoe than in the grounds of a horse trainer on the day of a pony jumping charity event? There were horseshoes everywhere. I simply had to have somebody on the inside search it out. I couldn't risk having a full scale search take place without giving the game away. Fortunately, it looks as if my contact has come up trumps."

Janice looked at her boss's smug expression and was certain this was all bullshit, or horse-shit at least. On the other hand, though, if this horseshoe was the murder weapon and had indeed been discovered at Strathbole Castle then she had to hand it to him for linking the two murders and thereby closing in on the murderer.

"I see," was as far as she was prepared to massage his ego at this point though.

After a long wait with Jimmy spouting more of the same the telephone eventually rang.

"Hello. Ruth?" demanded Jimmy.

"Yes, 'tis me," Ruth answered, clearly in high spirits. "We have a match! The blood stains on the horseshoe are Billy's and the bent nail matches exactly the imprint of two of the wounds on his head. I am even prepared to speculate that he was kicked by a horse with no shoe on its hoof and then struck twice with force by someone using this horseshoe as a far from blunt instrument."

"Brilliant," said Jimmy almost wetting his pants with joy. "That gives me enough to interview his slimy Lordship again and see what his story is."

"No need."

"Why? Asked Jimmy.

"Because I even have prints on the murder weapon."

"It's probably just that clown Milne's."

"How did you know? I have quite a collection of them. Some are Billy Winkman's but I have clear prints of George Milne's too and a partial print of someone else."

"Who else?"

"No idea but you have two murders and two weapons, both with George Milne's prints on them and he was at both locations at the time. I can't really do any more of your job for you now, can I?"

"It isn't Milne. It looks like it is but it isn't. Run a check on the partial print if you can."

"Are you serious?" said Ruth and hung up after confirming the written report would be with Jimmy the following day and advising him to arrest George Milne while he was still in the country.

Janice looked at her boss having listened to the whole conversation on the speaker.

"What's all that about? It has to be Milne."

"No. No motive, and it was him who handed me the horseshoe. That's how his prints got on it, and the knife that killed Eric was one from George's act. He is stupid but he isn't that stupid. Nobody could be," said Jimmy, starting to have his doubts.

After a pause he walked over to his notice board.

"Of course we'll arrest Milne, but it wasn't him. If he didn't have a motive then it is pretty obvious who else did."

Janice knew what was coming and wasn't keen on her career prospects being tied to Jimmy's pet theory.

"Lord fucking Strathbole discovers years ago that his butler has been shagging his wife. He packs him off to darkest Germany and then watches his only begotten son grow up to be the spitting image of his ex-butler. For years he must have brooded about that and made his wife's life such a living hell that she takes to the bottle for comfort. Then he notices Ramsay at the Butler's Ball and snaps. He is smart enough to know he can't do it himself but is fortunate in having a grateful ex-con with a propensity for violence in his employ; enter Billy Winkman at short notice, who grabs a knife from 'Les Cortez' on the way to Ramsay's room and uses it to kill him. Lord Strathbole is sitting beside ACC Cooper on the stage at the time of the murder and for several hours afterwards is with him in the bar. He has a cast iron alibi who is a senior policeman and senior freemason. We are therefore meant to assume that Strathbole has to be innocent. Afterwards, he starts to worry about Billy blabbing after a dram or three, or perhaps Billy asks for a huge wage rise to keep quiet, and his Lordship decides to do away with him personally. He plans it for an occasion when horseshoes are flying around his fields like butterflies on a summer's day and invites Cooper back again as the safest alibi he knows. Cooper jumps at the chance of staying at the Castle with his wife and sprog for the weekend and would obviously now kill anyone who upset his new best pal Hamish. His Lordship chooses his moment and kills Billy, then hides the weapon in a bush, maybe having been disturbed or planning to move it later, but before he can, my man George Milne finds it and brings it to me. All I need now is to match the partial print to Strathbole. What do you think? Am I right or am I right?"

"You are right that Cooper will kill anyone who upsets his new best pal. That much is beyond any reasonable doubt. If you take this theory forward you'd better be right," said Janice, deeply concerned at the way things were going.

"I've thought about that too. I'm going to go back to the castle and find a way of getting his Lordship's prints on something. If we can get a match to the partial print on the horseshoe then I'll have the bastard and Cooper will have to find a new pal at the Lodge to brown nose."

"How do you plan to do that?" asked Janice.

"I haven't quite figured that bit out yet but we can improvise when we get there."

"We?"

"Oh, yes, Janice, we. Two heads are better than one, safety in numbers, whatever way you want to put it, but we are both going to the castle and between us we are not leaving till we get a set of Lord Strathbole's prints."

With that he grabbed his car keys and coat and indicated that she should follow him.

"No time like the present," he said.

Janice reluctantly stood up and made her way to the door.

"Milne just happened to find that horseshoe, didn't he?" she asked.

"Eh, yes, actually," admitted her boss. "A pure stroke of luck really."

Chapter Fifty Two: Closing in on Hamish

Jimmy and his assistant arrived at Strathbole Castle late in the afternoon and drove straight to the front door. The towering building cast a shadow on Jimmy's car as he parked it. Janice looked round at the building and its grounds and felt no more comfortable about arriving unannounced to try to prove that its owner was a double murderer. She could see the logic in Jimmy's theory when he explained it in his office but here it was all a bit too… well… intimidating.

Jimmy strode over to the door and pulled the lever which rang the bell. After a few minutes' wait, during which Jimmy rang the bell a second time, the door was opened by Andrew the butler. He looked them up and down and at the grubby Vauxhall Vectra parked in the drive and said, "Can I help you?" in a way which suggested they might have failed to find the tradesman's entrance.

"Inspector Bell and Sergeant Young. I wonder if we might have a word with Lord Strathbole if he is in?"

"I will check," said Andrew, only slightly thrown at finding out two police officers wanted to interview his employer.

"It's official business, in connection with the recent death of Mr Winkman," added Jimmy to emphasise that Lord Strathbole should appear if he was anywhere in the vicinity.

"Very well, Inspector, please wait here," said Andrew recognising the tone in Jimmy's voice.

Janice looked round the wooden panelling of the inner hall and was impressed.

"You don't get this at B&Q," she said.

"It's all show to intimidate us plebs, remember. Keep your eyes open and watch for any reaction from his Lordship. I'm going to try and scare the shit out of him."

"Best of luck," thought Janice, looking at the collection of ancient weaponry hung round the castle walls.

After a long wait Andrew reappeared and said that Lord Strathbole would see them in his office, and led the way to a rather functional looking room near the kitchens. Lord Strathbole was sitting behind his desk when they were shown in and looked up from a farming map as they arrived in a way which suggested they were interrupting him and had better not waste too much of his valuable time.

"Sorry to interrupt," said Jimmy. "I appreciate you are busy and we won't take up any more of your time than we have to."

"I hope not inspector. I had rather thought poor Billy's accident would have been done and dusted by now."

"Part of the reason for our visit is to let you know we are now treating his death as suspicious and have begun a murder investigation."

Both police officers watched for any reaction at this news and were rewarded with just a hint of fear briefly flashing across their host's face. He swallowed involuntarily, before continuing.

"I'll have the horse handcuffed and brought round to the station if you like. Surely it is a clear cut case of him being kicked to death by an injured horse? I have the vet's report on the leg and the farrier's bill if you need proof."

There was a slight hint of concern in the voice which was now only just masked by the usual arrogance of its owner.

"The forensics suggest he was kicked by the horse and then struck with a large horseshoe; one unconnected to a horse. Have you any idea who might have done that?"

Lord Strathbole was now looking quite nervous and, having rising to his feet, made his way over to a tray of drinks on a shelf at the side of the room. Pouring himself a large whisky he offered the police officers a drink too, assuming they would not while on duty. To his and Janice's surprise, Jimmy accepted the offer and was passed a similar measure in a tumbler. Lord Strathbole took a large sip and looked thoughtful for a moment before replying.

"I can't think why anyone here would attack Billy, if that is indeed what happened. I know he had a history of violence, even while he was in jail. Perhaps one of his old victims tracked him down here."

As he spoke Hamish played with the tumbler in his hands nervously and quickly finished the drink in two further gulps. Jimmy had stood up with his, as yet, untouched glass and made a show of looking at the field maps on the walls while Janice took over the questioning. She wasn't sure what her boss had in mind but he was up to something and needed her to keep things flowing.

"I have to ask you where you were on the night that Billy was murdered, that was the night before the charity fund raising event for pony owners."

"Really. I think you better watch what you are doing here. I was dining with your Assistant Chief Constable

Brian Cooper, as you well know, and he can vouch for me again should you unwisely feel that is necessary."

"This is just routine to establish who was where, when Billy was killed. Can I ask what you were doing during the day before dinner? Again it's just routine, your Lordship."

Lord Strathbole looked more angry than worried now, even if it was an act, and put his empty glass down beside the drinks tray before going back to his desk to check his diary. As he did so Jimmy saw his chance. He poured the contents of his own glass into a plant pot near where he had been standing, then took the few steps towards the drinks tray where he quickly pocketed the glass which Lord Strathbole had been handling nervously until only a few seconds before.

Janice had followed their host to his desk diary and was largely masking Jimmy's movements where she was standing. After hearing the details of meetings and visits in the grounds from Lord Strathbole she thanked him and turned to her boss.

"Was there anything else you wanted to ask at the moment, Sir?"

"No, that's it really," said Jimmy casually. "I was sure you would prefer to hear the new nature of the enquiry from a senior officer. That's why I came at once to let you know personally."

"I appreciate that Inspector," said Hamish, having largely recovered his composure. "I hope you're wrong about Billy's death. It all sounds rather unpleasant."

"I wish I was, your Lordship, but the forensics are pretty conclusive."

As Janice and Jimmy reached the door of the office Jimmy turned and added, "We have a statement that Eric Ramsay once worked here many years ago. I wonder if you might check your records to see if that is true. Thank you again, Lord Strathbole. We'll see ourselves out."

The two police officers made their way back to the front door having again witnessed a fleeting look of fear on Lord Strathbole's face.

"I've got the bastard now," Jimmy thought as they headed to the car for a fast drive to Ruth Swanson's lab.

"You drive, Janice; I've some calls to make," Jimmy said as he threw his car keys at her. She missed them but quickly grabbed them from the gravel driveway, opened the car and jumped in, not quite sure what had just happened.

Back in his office a worried Lord Strathbole decided he had better make a few phone calls and ensure this snotty little policeman was stopped in his tracks. Events were taking a rather worrying turn and he knew just the person to speak to. He walked over to the drinks cabinet to pour himself another large whisky before phoning ACC Cooper to complain about the cheek of two of his officers, but the glass was not where he had left it.

"Strange," he thought, before taking another off the tray and filling it to the brim.

<u>Chapter Fifty Three : Crystal Clear</u>

Once they were heading at speed out of the castle grounds, Janice looked round at her boss.

"So exactly what just happened there? If he gave anything away I missed it, beyond a guilty look on his face; and when did you start drinking on duty?"

"I never touched a drop. I may have poisoned one of his pot plants though," said Jimmy as he produced Lord Strathbole's glass tumbler from his pocket and placed it carefully into an evidence bag. "With a bit of luck we will have a match on here to the partial print Ruth found on the horseshoe. If we don't we're both fucked and will be doing school crossings by the end of the week."

Janice sneaked a look at the tumbler and whistled.

"You sneaky bastard. You won't be able to use that in court, though."

"I won't have to. If we get a match we can drive straight back and arrest the bugger, taking his aristocratic prints even if we have to cut his fingers off to get them. In the meantime we need Ruth to check this before Cooper finds out and pulls us off the case."

"You think Strathbolc will try that?"

"I would bet my pension that our Hamish is phoning his old pal Brian Cooper at this very moment. We need to get this to Ruth and make ourselves scarce till we get an answer. Do you have any shopping you need to do? I'm going to pop in and visit my mother till Ruth phones me. I haven't seen her for ages. Don't answer your phone to anyone except me, and certainly not to ACC Cooper."

The rest of the journey passed in silence as both of the police officers considered what they might do for a living if the prints didn't match and they had got it all horribly wrong. When they arrived at the lab, Ruth was ready and waiting for them, and promised a quick result. After that Jimmy dropped Janice off in Princes Street before heading to Harthill to visit his rather surprised mother. Her son visiting her at all was unusual but during the working day was unheard of, and with service station flowers to boot; she did feel special.

Jimmy made small talk and listened to his mother bring him up to date with all his relatives, while nervously watching his phone. As he had anticipated, the phone soon rang with a call from his superintendent which had no doubt been instigated by ACC Cooper. His mother suggested she didn't mind if he answered it, but he minded, and once the first call rang out, he switched the phone to silent and tried to look interested in the details of his Uncle John's gall bladder operation.

The phone had rung again almost as soon as the first attempt to reach him failed and this time kept ringing for over twenty minutes. Again Jimmy nervously ignored his boss. The same happened three more times before the phone went dead for a few minutes. Then it lit up again but this time with ACC Cooper's number showing on it. Jimmy had long since lost the thread of his mother's story but kept smiling at her in a fixed way to encourage her to continue talking. Sitting beside his mother was somehow comforting, as all hell broke loose in Police Scotland while his superiors tried to contact him.

A text came through from Janice which simply said:"Shit, we're dead."

Eventually his phone rang with Ruth's office number showing on it.

"Well?" asked Jimmy when he answered it, now fearful for both his job and pension.

"Snap," said Ruth. "I have a match with the glass and the partial print on the horseshoe. I can confirm they almost certainly belong to the same person."

"Thanks Ruth, I owe you one," said Jimmy.

"No," said Ruth. "You owe me two dinners. Good luck."

Jimmy phoned Janice who had been too nervous to continue shopping when her phone had started ringing with calls from senior brass looking for her and for Jimmy, and she was trying to relax in a coffee shop.

"We've got him. The prints match. They both belong to our Hamish. I'll head over to see Cooper, who probably has a chopper out looking for me, and you arrive at the office in an hour's time. Anyone asks and you were at the library checking out Strathbole's background for me, and the librarian insisted your phone was off."

Jimmy kissed his mother goodbye and headed for his car. When he got there his phone rang again with ACC Cooper's number and he answered it.

"DI Bell"

"Not for long it won't be," shouted Cooper. "Where the bloody hell have you been, apart from harassing a peer of the realm?"

"Sorry, I've been out and about and struggling for a signal," said Jimmy as casually as possible.

"You'll be struggling for employment shortly. I want you in my office in half an hour and don't expect a cup of coffee and biscuits waiting for you when you get there."

Jimmy watched the call end on his phone and drove off, waving at his bemused mother as he went. Although his blood pressure was probably still close to terminal, he was starting to calm a bit. He had enough evidence to bring in Strathbole whether Cooper liked it or not. It might not be quite enough for an easy conviction in court, but it was enough to convince him that he had found a double murderer. The fact that the chief suspect was a close, personal friend of a shit like Cooper was just the icing on the cake.

Arriving at headquarters, he parked his car and made his way to ACC Cooper's office. His PA saw Jimmy approaching and turned pale before indicating with a wave of farewell that he was history, unless he had an unbelievably good excuse for harassing a friend of the ACC and disappearing for four hours during the day.

"I went to see my mum," he whispered as he passed her.

"Pull the other one," she whispered back before adding in a louder voice, "Just go in, ACC Cooper is waiting for you."

"Good afternoon, Sir, you wanted to see me?" said Jimmy as calmly as he could.

"Don't come the smart Alex with me, Bell. Why didn't you answer your bloody phone when I needed to talk to you?"

"I was visiting an old source. The signal's bad where they live."

"For four hours?"

"She had a lot to tell me. I've learned a great deal of useful stuff from her over the years."

"And where was that assistant of yours? I couldn't get hold of her either."

"She was leafing through some new material, I believe," said Jimmy with a degree of honesty.

Cooper brushed the explanation aside and launched into a long tirade of complaints about Bell's harassment of a prominent citizen, "A personal friend of mine", etc, etc, his failure to recognise a murder when he saw one (another inconvenience to his friend) and his dereliction of duty by not answering his phone. Jimmy weathered the storm waiting for the ideal opportunity to take the wind out of Cooper's sales. Eventually it arrived;

"What do you have to say for yourself?" Cooper demanded as he paused for breath.

"Lord Strathbole killed Billy Winkman."

Cooper's pause for breath became a struggle for oxygen.

"Have you lost what little there was of your mind? I was at dinner with him when Winkman died. Have you forgotten that?"

"No, Sir. Winkman died approximately three hours after being struck twice with an offensive weapon. The blows were struck before your party gathered for dinner. Unless you spent the late afternoon with his Lordship, he has no alibi for the time of the attack, only for the time of Billy's eventual and slow death."

"This is nonsense, Bell."

"We have Strathbole's prints on the weapon."

"Why on earth would Hamish Strathbole bludgeon his groom to death? Especially after all the winners he has trained for him."

Jimmy was warming to his task now and was determined to enjoy every moment as he slowly spun out the evidence to date.

"It was Billy Winkman's blood on the weapon which killed Eric Ramsay. I believe he killed Ramsay on the orders of Lord Strathbole."

"I suppose you have an explanation for that."

"Yes Sir. Ramsay was the real father of Simon Peter Strathbole, and his lordship found that out. We have confirmed this through DNA samples."

Cooper said nothing for a moment, clearly starting to listen seriously to what his subordinate was saying.

"Go on," he encouraged after a pause.

"I believe that Lord Strathbole saw red when he found out that his ex-butler had fathered his only son and heir. He persuaded or blackmailed Billy Winkman into killing Ramsay and then took the first opportunity to get rid of him, hoping that the horse would take the blame. He deliberately used you as an alibi on each occasion but misjudged how long it would take for poor Billy to die."

"What is the evidence against him?" said Cooper now quietly listening without a hint of interruption.

"At the Pacific Hotel, he gave a statement denying any knowledge of Eric Ramsay, despite the fact that he had worked as his butler for five years. We have his fingerprint on the horseshoe that was used to kill Billy Winkman, a horseshoe which was found hidden under a bush between the stable block and the Strathbole castle. I have enough to bring him in and interview him under caution as a suspect. He lied to me and he used you, Sir. I think he deserves a visit to the local station, don't you?"

Cooper was deep in thought. It all sounded very plausible now, the way that Jimmy explained it. Losing a peer of the realm as a friend would be a blow, and being his guest at both murders to provide an alibi on each occasion would not be the career-enhancing contact he had hoped for. His wife would also not be pleased and he had no idea how he was going to explain things at his Golf Club.

"You'd better be right about this Bell. I don't want this to go pear-shaped when the press get hold of it. Have you interviewed young Simon Strathbole yet? This will all come as a huge shock to him if it's true."

"No, Sir. I believe he is visiting friends or family in Germany at the moment, something about a recent bereavement."

"Okay, Bell. Tread wearily with this one. I can't help you if you mess it up, and the press will have your guts for garters. Now go and get him."

"Thank you, Sir," said Jimmy trying to remove all possible hint of sarcasm from his voice.

Once he had left the office, Cooper picked up the phone to his PA. "Hold any calls from Lord Strathbole, Jenny. If he does phone I'm in a meeting. Yes, every time he phones I will be in a meeting, whether I am or not."

Chapter Fifty Four: Hamish gets his collar felt

Jimmy headed for his office on an adrenalin high. He had been right about Strathbole and had watched Cooper almost, if not quite, have to eat his words and apologise. It had come as close to that as it would ever do. Cooper wasn't the apologising kind but he had been forced to shut up and listen before agreeing that Jimmy was right. That would do for now.

Janice was waiting in his office with a look of serious concern on her face.

"Well?" she asked nervously.

"We've got the go ahead to bring in that bastard Strathbole and question him about the murders of Eric Ramsay and Billy Winkman under caution."

"How was Cooper?"

"Strathbole had obviously got to him, but he had to shut up and listen now we have a match on the murder weapon. Let's go and get Hamish and make him sweat."

"How was your mother, by the way?"

"Good thanks. Buy any nice clothes?"

"Just a top for the beach, thanks."

"Good day all round, then. Now let's go get him."

Jimmy and Janice arrived at Strathbole Castle as the light was fading and drove straight to the main door. Jimmy again rang the bell as loudly as he could and was surprised when Lady Fiona Strathbole answered.

"Inspector Bell, isn't it?" she asked.

"Yes it is. I need to talk to your husband. Is he in?"

"Yes, he is in the study trying to contact that dreadful man Cooper. I assume you are here to arrest him for killing Eric Ramsay?"

Jimmy was even more surprised at this question.

"I need to speak to him about that, yes, and about Billy Winkman's murder. Do you know anything about these things?"

"Yes, Inspector. Hamish told me all about it. Taunted me really. He is a beast. He told me he arranged for Eric's death. He'd found out about poor Simon and decided to get rid of Eric. He shouted at me that he had done it. Poor Eric. He was so kind to me when I needed a friend."

"Are you prepared to testify against your husband to that effect in a court of law?"

"Yes, Inspector, I believe I am now," said Lady Fiona. "My friends at Alcoholics Anonymous have given me so much strength and confidence. It is the least I can do for Eric."

Jimmy turned to Janice who had her note book at the ready and gave him a thumbs up to confirm that she was on it.

Jimmy continued through the Castle to the study where he had so recently met Lord Strathbole.

His Lordship was sitting behind the large desk in the office with a large whisky in his hand.

"I don't suppose you will join me this time, Inspector?" he said as Jimmy entered the office.

"No thank you, Sir. I never drink on duty."

"So I realise, now," said Lord Strathbole.

"You'll get your glass back eventually. I am arresting you for the murder of Billy Winkman and for conspiracy to murder Eric Ramsay."

Jimmy went on to tell him his rights.

"You don't have enough to jail me," said Strathbole.

"I think we do, actually. Now that your wife is prepared to testify against you."

Lord Strathbole suddenly looked up at Jimmy.

"I doubt if she will make much of a witness even if she manages to show up sober. Men like me don't go to prison, inspector."

<u>Chapter Fifty Five: Tidy Up</u>

When Lord Strathbole was sent to prison for the murder of his groom, William Winkman and his former butler Eric Ramsay, the press had a field day. The conviction and jailing of Lord Strathbole was all over the newspapers from the day of his arrest till he was sentenced to life with a minimum of 18 years. ACC Cooper was interviewed on the steps of the High Court taking all the credit he could. It was spoiled slightly by a regional reporter who asked him how he felt about seeing an old friend convicted of murder.

Jimmy and Janice were commended for their efforts by their superintendent, who had been briefed by ACC Cooper to keep them away from the High Court on the day of sentencing.

Jimmy sent a thank you card to George, along with a clown's nose. The message in the card read, "Thank you. Now stop clowning around."

In Germany Kurt followed the trial on a daily basis, constantly waiting for a knock on the Schloss door which never came. At least Hamish kept quiet about his involvement in setting Eric up. Otto had grown distant from Kurt recently and was spending more and more time at the Summer House in Alsace. He was joined there on a regular basis by young Simon Peter Strathbole who had surprised the British press by not attending his father's trial. The two young men seemed to have grown close and had been of great comfort to Eric's widow and her daughters.

Lola headed off to Europe after the trial, with Benny still dodging the knives, having left his wife and family for the uncertainties of Lola's blossoming stage career.

Janine had moved out of George's house by the time he returned as she had promised and showed no immediate sign of returning.

Chapter Fifty Six: Back to the old routine

On the day after Lord Strathbole was sentenced, George made himself a large mug of coffee in his favourite mug, popped the spoon into the sink of unwashed dishes and took two chocolate digestives from the opened packet next to the kettle. Carrying the drink, the biscuits and the mail he had collected from the door mat he made his way through to his favourite chair in the front room. His favourite chair was once again his favourite chair. The sofa generally sat unoccupied these days unless Evelyn was dropped off at his house before Rosie and Carol went out on the town. Otherwise it lay quiet and empty. Gone were the days of Zebra clad girls and women sprawled across its fading fabric. George regretted this loss in his life more than most things but along with the loss came the return of peace and tranquillity and the return of the boredom he had once grown to enjoy after his separation and divorce from Glenda.

It was true that he had enjoyed at least some moments of the adventurous life he found himself living from time to time, and he genuinely missed Janine's company and companionship, but there was only so much excitement someone like George could expect or indeed cope with in a lifetime. He felt that he had had his fill and perhaps more, and that if life now returned to a mundane level then he could make do with that till his days were done. Too much excitement and adventure was for other people; people like Jimmy Bell, Lola Cortez and the other circus acts he had met who were born for it. Even people like Lord Hamish Strathbole. He was not though, and never would be.

He looked at the small bundle of mail, recognising the usual suspects of a phone bill, and two unsolicited leaflets; one for double glazing and the other for a local discount supermarket. At the bottom of the pile, however, was something unusual and unexpected: a postcard. The picture was of Monte Carlo with an expensive collection of private yachts ranged round the old harbour. He turned it over and read the message on the back.

"Dear George,

We are touring the world, starting with Europe, and have a private booking with local royalty, one of whom saw my act elsewhere and liked what he saw (Ha, ha!). I have hit Benny only once with my knives since we left Scotland but have been tempted to do so on many other occasions. He tries hard but he lacks your comic timing. Don't believe what anyone says about you, George; you are only ever a clown when you want to be and then you are the world's best.

I don't know how long I will be touring and suspect Benny may have to be replaced soon. Rest assured I will look you up the next time I am in Scotland and you can assess my dirty dancing once more.

Love, kisses and more

Lola xxx"

George felt quite warm and special for a moment after he read it and placed the card on top of his mantelpiece. He may find himself alone for the moment but the card held the slight and distant chance of future adventures. Perhaps it might also promise further romance, he thought wistfully. Just not for a few years, he hoped, and turned on the television news.

THE END

The Treasure Hunters

A small and apparently sleepy village becomes the focus in the search for missing CIA funds. Someone local has 'got rich quick' but the security services can't broadcast their loss without admitting what is going on nearby and have to try to discover who without raising any suspicions. Robbie Buchanan is blackmailed out of medical retirement to track down the cash, but has his training in MI6 prepared him for everything the village of Kirkton has in store?

Roddy Murray's third book takes a riotous route through village life as cultures clash and the big, wide world meets its match.

The permutations of who was living or sleeping with whom and who had previously been living or sleeping with who else seemed endless according to some people's accounts. Robbie was glad, however, for the piece of advice Jennifer had given him about arriving in a small village: "Always assume you are talking to someone related to whoever you are talking about and you won't go far wrong."

Body and Soul

Two very different men are on a pathway to a meeting which will change both their lives forever. One is a Scottish ex-soldier, ex-boxer, ex-husband, ex-father and ex-drunk struggling to turn his life around. The other, the CEO of an American multi-national, has both wealth and power. They do not know each other and only the American believes he knows the true purpose of their meeting. In fact both have been duped in different ways and as their lives begin to unravel they must try to deal with the truth if they can. Only one has the skills and determination to survive.

After failing to wake Frank he dragged him into the shower which conveniently only produced cold water and turned it on full. The effect wasn't immediate, but slowly the old fighting, kicking Frank began to re-appear, curse the first house guest he had had for six months and try to throw him out. After an initial but futile attempt to punch Paddy's lights out Frank calmed down enough to recognise his visitor.

Made in the USA
Charleston, SC
09 July 2016